The Pace That Kills: A Ch

By
Edgar Saltus

PART I.

I.

"I wish you a happy New Year, sir."

It was the servant, green of livery, the yellow waistcoat slashed with black, bearing the coffee and fruit.

"Put it there, please," Roland answered. And then, in recognition of the salutation, he added, "Thanks: the same to you."

"H'm," he mused, as the man withdrew, "I ought to have tipped him, I suppose."

He leaned from the bed, poured some milk into a cup, and for a second nibbled at a slice of iced orange. Through the transom came a faint odor of home-made bread, and with it the rustle of a gown and a girl's clear laugh. The room itself was small. It was furnished in a fashion which was unsuggestive of an hotel, and yet did not resemble that of a private house. The curtain had been already drawn. Beyond was a lake, very blue in the sunlight, bulwarked by undulant hills. Below, on the road, a dogcart fronted by a groom was awaiting somebody's pleasure.

"It is late," he reflected, and raised a napkin to his lips. As he did so he noticed a package of letters which the napkin must have concealed. He took up the topmost and eyed it. It had been addressed to the Athenæum Club, Fifth Avenue; but the original direction was erased, and Tuxedo Park inserted in its stead. On the upper left-hand corner the impress of a firm of tailors shone in blue. Opposite was the engraving of a young woman supported by 2-1/2d. He put it down again and glanced at the others. The superscriptions were characterless enough; each bore a foreign stamp, and to one as practised as was he, each bore the token of the dun.

"If they keep on bothering me like this," he muttered, "I shall certainly place the matter in the hands of my attorney." And thereat, with the air of a man who had said something insultingly original, he laughed aloud, swallowed some coffee, and dashed his head in the pillow. In and out of the corners of his mouth a smile still played; but presently his fancy must have veered, for the muscles of his lips compressed, and as he lay there, the arms clasped behind the head, the pink silk of his sleeves framing and tinting his face, and in the eyes the expression of one prepared to meet Fate and outwit it, a possible observer who could have chanced that way would have sat himself down to study and risen up perplexed.

Anyone who was at Columbia ten years ago will remember Roland Mistrial,—Roland Mistrial 3d, if you please,—and will recall the wave of bewilderment which swept the campus when that young gentleman, on the eve of graduation, popularity on one side and honors on the other, suddenly, without so much as a p. p. c., left everything where it was and betook himself to other shores. The flight was indeed erratic, and numerous were the rumors which it excited; but Commencement was at hand, other issues were to be considered, bewilderment subsided as bewilderment ever does, the college dispersed, and when it assembled again the Mistrial mystery, though unelucidated, was practically forgot.

In the neighborhood of Washington Square, however, on the northwest corner of Tenth Street and Fifth Avenue to be exact, there were others whose memories were more retentive. Among them was Roland's grandfather, himself a graduate, founder of the Mistrial fellowship, and judge of the appellate court. And there was Roland's father, a graduate too, a gentleman widely respected, all the more so perhaps because he had run for the governorship and lost it. And again there was Roland's aunt, a maiden lady of whom it is recorded that each day of her life she got down on her knees and thanked God he had made her a Mistrial. In addition to these, there were, scattered along the Hudson, certain maternal relatives—the Algaroths, the Baxters, and the Swifts; Bishop Algaroth in particular, who possessed such indomitable vigor that when at the good old age of threescore and ten he decided to depart this life, the impression prevailed that he had died very young for him. None of these people readily forgot. They were a proud family and an influential one—influential not merely in the social sense, but influential in political, legal, in church and university circles as well; a fact which may have had weight with the Faculty when it was called upon to deal with Roland Mistrial 3d. But be that as it may, the cause of the young man's disappearance was never officially given. Among the rumors which it created was one to the effect that his health was affected; in another his mind was implicated; and in a third it was his heart. Yet as not one of these rumors had enough evidential value behind it to concoct an anonymous letter on, they were suffered to go their way undetained, very much as Roland had already gone his own.

That way led him straight to the Golden Gate and out of it to Japan. Before he reached Yeddo his grandfather left the planet and a round sum of money behind. Of that round sum the grandson came in for a portion. It was not fabulous in dimensions, but in the East money goes far. In this case it might have gone on indefinitely had not the beneficiary seen fit to abandon the languors of the Orient for the breezier atmosphere of the west. The Riviera has charms of its own. So, too, have Paris and Vienna. Roland enjoyed them to the best of his ability. He even found London attractive, and became acclimated in Pall Mall. In the latter region he learned one day that his share of the round sum had departed and his father as well. The conjunction of these incidents was of such a character that he at once took ship for New York.

It was not that he was impatient to revisit the misgoverned city which he had deserted ten years before. He had left it willingly enough, and he had seldom regretted it since. The pins and needles on which he sat were those of another make. He was uninformed of the disposition of his father's property, and he felt that, were not every penny of it bequeathed to him, he would be in a tight box indeed.

He was at that time just entering his thirtieth year—that age in which a man who has led a certain life begins to be particular about the quality of his red pepper, and anxious too that the supply of it shall not tarry. Though meagre of late, the supply had been sufficient. But at present the palate was a trifle impaired. Where a ten-pound note had sufficed for its excitement, a hundred now were none too strong. Roland Mistrial—3d no longer—wanted money, and he wanted plenty of it. He had exact ideas as to its usefulness, and none at all regarding its manufacture. He held, as many have done and will continue to do, that the royal road to it leads through a testament; and it was in view of the opening vistas which that road displayed that he set sail for New York.

And now, six weeks later, on this fair noonday of a newer year, as he lay outstretched in bed, you would have likened him to one well qualified to keep a mother awake and bring her daughter dreams. Our canons of beauty may be relative, but, such as they are, his features accorded with them—disquietingly even; for they conveyed the irritating charm of things we have hoped for, striven for, failed to get, and then renounced with thanksgiving. They made you anxious about their possessor, and fearful too lest the one dearly-beloved might chance to see them, and so be subjugated by their spell. They were features that represented good stock, good breeding, good taste, good looks—every form of goodness, in fact, save, it may be, the proper one. But the possible lack of that particular characteristic was a matter over which hesitation well might be. We have all of us a trick of flattering ourselves with the fancy that, however obtuse our neighbor is, we at least are gifted with the insight of a detective—a faculty so rare and enviable that the blunders we make must be committed with a view to its concealment; yet, despite presumable shrewdness, now and then a face will appear that eludes cataloguing, and leaves the observer perplexed. Roland Mistrial's was one of these.

And now, as the pink silk of his shirt-sleeves tinted it, the expression altered, and behind his contracted brows hurried processions of shifting scenes. There was that initial catastrophe which awaited him almost on the wharf—the discovery that his father had left him nothing, and that for no other reason in the world than because he had nothing whatever to leave—nothing, in fact, save the hereditary decoration of and right of enrolment in the Society of the Cincinnati, the which, handed down since Washingtonian days from one Mistrial to another, he held, as his forefathers had before him, in trust for the Mistrials to be.

No, he could not have disposed of that, even had he so desired; but everything else, the house on Tenth Street,—built originally for a country-seat, in times when the Astor House was considered rather far uptown,—bonds, scrip, and stocks, disappeared as utterly as had they never been; for Roland's father, stricken with that form of dementia which, to the complete discouragement of virtue, battens on men that have led the chastest lives, had, at that age in which the typical rake is forced to haul his standard down, surrendered himself to senile debauchery, and in the lap of a female of uncertain attractions—of whose mere existence no one had been previously aware—placed title-deeds and certificates of stock. In a case such as this the appeal of the rightful heir is listened to with such patience that judge and jury too have been known to pass away and leave the tale unended. And Roland, when the earliest dismay had in a measure subsided, saw himself closeted with lawyers who offered modicums of hope in return for proportionate fees. Then came a run up the Hudson, the welcomeless greeting which waited him there, and the enervating imbecility of his great aunt, whose fingers, mummified by gout, were tenacious enough on the strings of her purse. That episode flitted by, leaving on memory's camera only the degrading tableau of coin burrowed for and unobtained. And through it all filtered torturesome uncertainties, the knowledge of his entire inability to make money, the sense of strength misspent, the perplexities that declined to take themselves away, forebodings of the morrow, nay of the day even as well, the unbanishable dread of want.

But that for the moment had gone. He turned on his elbow and glanced over at a card-case which lay among the silver-backed brushes beyond, and at once the shock he had resummoned fled. Ah, yes! it had gone indeed, but at the moment it had been appalling enough. The morrow at least was secure; and as he pondered over its possibilities they faded before certain episodes of the previous day—that chance encounter with Alphabet Jones, who had insisted he should pack a valise and go down with Trement Yarde and himself to Tuxedo; and at once the incidents succeeding the arrival paraded through his thoughts. There had been the late dinner to begin with; then the dance; the girl to whom some one had presented him, and with whom he had sat it out; the escape of the year, the health that was drunk to the new one, and afterwards the green baize in the card-room; the bank which Trement Yarde had held, and finally the successful operation that followed, and which consisted in cutting that cherub's throat to the tune of three thousand dollars. It was all there now in the card-case; and though, as sums of money go, it was hardly quotable, yet in the abstract, forethought and economy aiding, it represented several months of horizons solid and real. The day was secure; as for the future, who knew what it might contain? A grave perhaps, and in it his aunt.

II.

"If I had been killed in a duel I couldn't be better." It was Jones the novelist describing the state of his health. "But how is my friend and brother in virtue?"

"Utterly ramollescent," Roland answered, confidingly. "What the French call gaga."

The mid-day meal was in progress, and the two men, seated opposite each other, were dividing a Demidorf salad. They had been schoolmates at Concord, and despite the fact that until the day before they had not met for a decennium, the happy-go-lucky intimacy of earlier days had eluded Time and still survived. Throughout the glass-enclosed piazza other people were lunching, and every now and then Jones, catching a wandering eye, would bend forward a little and smile. Though it was but the first of the year, the weather resembled that of May. One huge casement was wide open. There was sunlight everywhere, flowers too, and beyond you could see the sky, a dome of opal and sapphire blent.

"Well," Jones replied, "I can't say you have altered much. But then who does? You remember, don't you"—and Jones ran on with some anecdote of earlier days.

But Roland had ceased to listen. It was very pleasant here, he told himself. There was a freedom about it that the English country-house, however charming, lacked. There was no one to suggest things for you to do, there was no host or hostess to exact attention, and the women were prettier, better dressed, less conventional, and yet more assured in manner than any that he had encountered for years. The men, too, were a good lot; and given one or two more little surprises, such as he had found in the card-room, he felt willing to linger on indefinitely—a week at least, a month if the fare held out. His eyes roamed through the glitter of the room. Presently, at a neighboring table, he noticed the girl with whom he had seen the old year depart: she was nodding to him; and Roland, with that courtesy that betokens the foreigner a mile away, rose from his seat as he bowed in return.

Jones, whom little escaped, glanced over his shoulder. "By the way, are you on this side for good?" he asked; and Roland answering with the vague shrug the undetermined give, he hastened to add—"or for bad?"

"That depends. I ran over to settle my father's estate, but they seem to have settled it for me. After all, this is no place for a pauper, is it?"

"The wolf's at the door, is he?"

Roland laughed shortly. "At the door? Good Lord! I wish he were! He's in the room."

"There, dear boy, never mind. Wait till spring comes and marry an heiress. There are so many hereabouts that we use them for export purposes. They are a glut in the market. There's a fair specimen. Ever meet her before?"

"Meet whom?"

"That girl you just bowed to. They call her father Honest Paul. Oh, if you ask me why, I can't tell. It's a nick-name, like another. It may be because he says Amen so loud in church. A number of people have made him trustee, but whether on that account or not they never told. However, he's a big man, owns a mile or two up there near the Riverside. I should rate him at not a penny less than ten million."

"What did you say his name was?"

"Dunellen—the Hon. Paul Dunellen. At one time—"

Jones rambled on, and again Roland had ceased to listen. But it was not the present now that claimed him. At the mention of the plutocrat something from the past came back and called him there—a thing so shadowy that, when he turned to interrogate, it eluded him and disappeared. Then at once, without conscious effort, an episode which he had long since put from him arose and detained his thought. But what on earth, he wondered, had the name of Dunellen to do with that? And for the moment dumbly perplexed, yet outwardly attentive, he puzzled over the connection and tried to find the link; yet that too was elusive: the name seemed to lose its suggestiveness, and presently it sank behind the episode it had evoked.

"Of course," Jones was saying, in reference, evidently, to what had gone before—"of course as millionaires go he is not first chop. Jerolomon could match him head or tail for all he has, and never miss it if he lost. Ten million, though, is a tidy sum—just enough to entertain on. A penny less and you are pinched. Why, you would be surprised—"

"Has he any other children?"

"Who? Dunellen? None that he has acknowledged."

"Then his daughter will come in for it all."

"That's what I said. When she does, she will probably hand it over to some man who wont know how to spend it. She's got a cousin—what's that beggar's name? However, he's a physician, makes a specialty of nervous diseases, I believe; good enough fellow in his way, but an everlasting bore—the sort of man you would avoid in a club, and trust your sister to. What the deuce is his name?"

"Well, what of him?"

"Ah, yes. I fancy he wants to get married, and when he does, to entertain. He is very devoted."

"But nowadays, barring royalty, no one ever marries a cousin."

"Dear boy, you forget; it isn't every cousin that has ten million. When she has, the attempt is invariable." And Jones accentuated his remark with a nod. "Now," he continued, "what do you say to a look at the library? They have a superb edition of Kirschwasser in there, and a full set of the works of Chartreuse."

The novelist had arisen; he was leaving the room, and Roland was about to follow him, when he noticed that Miss Dunellen was preparing to leave it too. Before she reached the hall he was at her side.

There is this about the New York girl—her beauty is often bewildering, yet unless a husband catch her in the nick of time the bewilderment of that beauty fades. At sixteen Justine Dunellen had been enchanting, at twenty-three she was plain. Her face still retained its oval, but from it something had evaporated and gone. Her mouth, too, had altered. In place of the volatile brilliance of earlier years, it was drawn a little; it seemed resolute, and it also seemed subdued. But one feature had not changed: her eyes, which were of the color of snuff, enchanted still. They were large and clear, and when you looked in them you saw such possibilities of tenderness and sincerity that the escape of the transient was unregretted; you forgot the girl that had been, and loved the woman that was.

And lovable she was indeed. The world is filled with charming people whom, parenthetically, many of us never meet; yet, however scant our list may be, there are moments when from Memory's gardens a vision issues we would fain detain. Who is there to whom that vision has not come? Nay, who is there that has not intercepted it, and, to the heart's perdition perhaps, suffered it to retreat? If there be any to whom such apparitions are unvouchsafed, let him evoke that woman whom he would like his sister to resemble and his wife to be. Then, if his intuitions are acute, there will appear before him one who has turned sympathy into a garment and taken refinement for a wreath; a woman just yet debonair, thoughtful of others, true to herself; a woman whose speech can weary no more than can a star, whose mind is clean as wholesome fruit, whose laugh is infrequent, and whose voice consoles; a woman who makes the boor chivalrous, and the chivalrous bend the knee. Such an one did Justine Dunellen seem. In person she was tall, slender, willowy of movement, with just that shrinking graciousness that the old masters gave to certain figures which they wished to represent as floating off the canvas into space.

And now, as Roland joined her, she smiled and greeted him. With her was a lady to whom she turned:

"Mrs. Metuchen, this is Mr. Mistrial."

And Roland found himself bowing to a little old woman elaborately dressed. She was, he presently discovered, a feather-head person, who gave herself the airs of a princesse en couches. But though not the rose, at least she dwelt near by. Her husband was Mr. Dunellen's partner; and to Justine, particularly since the death of her mother, she had become what the Germans, who have many a neat expression, term a Wahlverwandtschaft—a relation not of blood, but of choice. She was feather-headed, but she was a lady; she was absurd, but she was lovable; and by Justine she was evidently beloved.

Roland got her a seat, found a footstool for her, and pleased her very much by the interest which he displayed in her family tree.

"I knew all your people," she announced at last. And when she did so, her manner was so gracious that Roland felt the hour had not been thrown away.

During the rest of the day he managed to be frequently in her vicinity. The better part of the morrow he succeeded in sharing with Justine. And in the evening, when the latter bade him good-night, it occurred to him that if what

Jones had said in regard to the cousin was true, then was the cousin losing ground.

The next morning Mrs. Metuchen and her charge returned to town. Roland followed in a later train. As he crossed the ferry he told himself he had much to do; and on reaching New York he picked up his valise with the air of one who has no time to lose.

III.

In a city like New York it is not an easy task, nor is it always a profitable one, to besiege a young person that is fortressed in her father's house. And when the house has a cousin for sentinel, and that cousin is jealous, the difficulty is increased. But, time and tact aiding, what obstacle may not be removed?

Roland understood all this very thoroughly, and on the day succeeding his return from Tuxedo he examined the directory, strolled into Wall Street, and there, at the shingle of Dunellen, Metuchen, & Such, sent in a card to the senior member of the firm.

The Hon. Paul Dunellen—Honest Paul, to the world in which he moved—was a man who in his prime must have been of glad and gallant appearance; but latterly he had shrunk: his back had bent almost into a hump, he held his head lower than his shoulders, but with uplifted chin—a habit which gave him the appearance of being constantly occupied in peering at something which he could not quite discern, an appearance that was heightened by his eyes, which were restless, and by his brows, which were tormented and bushy. He had an ample mouth: when he spoke, the furrows in his cheeks moved with it. His nose was prominent; all his features, even to his ears, were larger than the average mould. When Roland was admitted to the room in which he sat, the first impression which he got from him was that of massiveness in decay.

"Mr. Mistrial, I am glad to see you. I knew your father, and I had the honor of knowing your grandfather as well. Will you not take a seat?" The old man had half risen, and in this greeting made manifest something of that courtesy which we are learning to forget.

"You are very kind," Roland answered. "It is because of my father that I venture to call. If I interrupt you, though"—and Roland, apparently hesitant, occupied himself in a study of his host—"if I do," he continued, "I beg you will allow me to come again."

To this suggestion Mr. Dunellen refused to listen; but during the moments that followed, as Roland succinctly one after the other enumerated the facts in the case of his lost inheritance, the lawyer did listen; and he listened, moreover, with that air of concentrated attention which is the surest encouragement to him who has aught to say. And when Roland had completed the tale of his grievance, he nodded, and stroked his chin.

"The matter is perfectly clear," he announced, "though I can't say as much for the law. Undue influence is evident. The trouble will be to invalidate a gift made during the lifetime of the donor; but—" And Mr. Dunellen made a gesture as who should say, It is for that that courts were established. "Yet, tell me, why is it that you have done nothing about it before?"

To this Roland made no immediate reply. He lowered his eyes. "Paralysis is written in your face," he mused. Then aloud and rather sadly: "The fairest patrimony is an honored name," he said. "It is for me to guard my father's reputation. It is only recently, stress of circumstances aiding, I have thought that without publicity some compromise might possibly be effected." He looked up again, and as he looked he assured himself that the old man would not outlast the year.

"Well, Mr. Mistrial, you must let me quote the speech a lord made to a commoner, 'You are not a noble, sir, but you are worthy of being one.'" And Mr. Dunellen reaching out caught Roland's hand and shook it in his own. "I enter thoroughly into your delicacy the more readily because I do not encounter it every day—no, nor every month. It does me good—on my word it does. Now, if a compromise can, as you suggest, be effected, and you care to leave the matter in my hands, I will do my best to serve you. It may take some little time, we must seem neither zealous nor impatient, and meanwhile—h'm—I understood you to say something about your circumstances. Now if I can be of any—"

This offer Roland interrupted. "You are truly very kind, sir," he broke in, "and I thank you with all my heart. All the more so even because I must refuse. I have been badly brought up, I know; you see, I never expected that it would be necessary for me to earn my own living; yet if it is, I cannot begin too soon: but what would the end be if I began by borrowing money?"

As Roland delivered this fine speech he was the image of Honesty arrayed in a Piccadilly coat. He rose from his seat. "I am detaining you, I am sure. Let me get the papers together and bring them to you to-morrow."

"Do so, by all means," Mr. Dunellen answered, rising too. "Do so, by all means. But wait: to-morrow I may be absent. Could you not send them to my house this evening, or better still, bring them yourself? It would give me pleasure to have my daughter meet a man who is the moral portrait of his grandfather."

"Your daughter!" Roland exclaimed. "It is not possible that she is the Miss Dunellen whom I saw the other day at Tuxedo."

"With Mrs. Metuchen? Why, of course it is." And the lawyer looked as surprised as his client. "This is indeed a coincidence. But you will come, will you not?"

"I shall consider it a privilege to do so," Roland, with a charming affectation of modesty, replied; and presently, when he found himself in the street again, he saw, stretching out into beckoning vistas, a high-road paved with promises of prompt success.

And that evening, when the papers had been delivered, and Mr. Dunellen, leaving the guest to his daughter's care, had gone with them to his study, Roland could not help but feel that on that high-road his footing was assured; for, on entering the drawing-room, Justine had greeted him as one awaited and welcome, and now that her father had gone she motioned him to a seat at her side.

"Tell me," she said, "what is it you do to people? There is Mrs. Metuchen, who pretends to abominate young men, and openly admires you. To-day you captured my father; by to-morrow you will be friends with Guy."

"With Guy?" Mechanically Roland repeated the phrase. Then at once into the very core of memory entered the lancinating pang of a nerve exposed. During the second that followed, in that tumult of visions that visits him who awakes from a swoon, there came to him the effort made in Tuxedo to recall in what manner the name of Dunellen was familiar to his ears; but that instantly departed, and in its stead came a face one blur of tears, and behind it a stripling livid with hate. Could that be Guy? If it were, then indeed would the high-road narrow into an alley, with a dead wall at the end. Yet of the inward distress he gave no outward sign. About his thin lips a smile still played, and as he repeated the phrase he looked, as he always did, confident and self-possessed.

"Yes, I am sure you will like each other," the girl answered; "all the more so perhaps because no two people could be less alike. Guy, you see, is—"

But whatever description she may have intended to give remained unexpressed. A portière had been drawn, and some one was entering the room. Roland, whose back was toward the door, turned obliquely and looked.

"Why, there he is!" he heard Justine exclaim; and in the man that stood there he saw the stripling he had just evoked. Into the palms of his hands a moisture came, yet as Justine proceeded with some form of introduction he rose to his feet. "So you are the cousin," he mused; and then, with a bow in which he put the completest indifference, he resumed his seat.

"We were just talking of you," Justine continued. "Why didn't you come in last night?"

"It is snowing," the cousin remarked, inconsequently, and sat himself down.

"Dr. Thorold, you know;" and Justine, turning to Mistrial, began to relate one of those little anecdotes which are serviceable when conversation drags.

As she ran on, Roland, apparently attentive, marked that one of Thorold's feet was moving uneasily, and divined rather than saw that the fingers of his hand were clinched. "He is working himself up," he reflected. "Well, let him; it will make it the easier for me." And as he told himself this he turned on Thorold a glance which he was prepared to instantly divert. But the physician was not looking; he sat bolt-upright, his eyes lowered, and about his mouth and forehead the creases of a scowl.

Dr. Thorold was of that class of man that women always like and never adore. He was thoughtful of others, and considerate. Physically he was well-favored, and pleasant to the eye. He was sometimes dull, but rarely selfish; by taste and training he was a scholar—gifted at that; and yet through some accident of nature he lacked that one fibre which differentiates the hero from the herd. In the way we live to-day the need of heroes is so slight that the absence of that fibre is of no moment at all—a circumstance which may account for the fact that Justine admired him very much, trusted him entirely, and had she been his sister instead of his cousin could not have appreciated him more.

And now, as Roland eyed him for one moment, through some of those indetectable currents that bring trivialities to the mind that is most deeply engrossed he noticed that though the physician was in dress the shoes he wore were not veneered. Then at once he entered into a perfect understanding of the circumstances in which he was placed. Though he lost the game even as the cards were being dealt, at least he would lose it well. "I'll teach him a lesson," he decided; and presently, as Justine ceased speaking, he assumed his gayest air.

"Yes, yes," he exclaimed, and gave a twist to his light mustache. He had caught her ultimate words, and with them a cue.

"Yes, I remember in Nepal—"

And thereupon he carried his listener through a series of scenes and adventures which he made graphic by sheer dexterity in the use of words. His speech, colored and fluent, was of exactly that order which must be heard, not read. It was his intonation which gave it its charm, the manner in which he eluded a detail that might have wearied; the expression his face took on at the situations which he saw before describing, and which he made his auditor expect; and also the surety of his skill in transition—the art with which he would pass from one idea to another, connect them both with a gesture, and complete the subject with a smile. The raconteur is usually a bore. When he is not, he is a wizard. And as Roland passed from one peak of the Himalayas to another, over one of the two that listened he exerted a palpable spell. At last, the end of his tether reached, he turned to the cousin, and, without a hesitation intervening, asked of him, as though the question were one of really personal interest, "Dr. Thorold, have you ever been in the East?"

Thorold, thrown off his guard, glared for an instant, the scowl still manifest; then he stood up. "No, sir; I have not," he answered; and each of the monosyllables of his reply he seemed to propel with tongue and teeth. "Good-night, Justine." And with a nod that was rather small for two to divide, took himself from the room.

He reached the portière before Justine fully grasped the discourtesy of his conduct. She stared after him wonderingly, her lips half parted, her clear eyes dilated and amazed, the color mounted to her cheeks, and she made as though to leave her seat.

But this Roland thought it wise to prevent. "Miss Dunellen," he murmured, "I am afraid Dr. Thorold was bored. It is my fault. I had no right—"

"Bored! How could he have been? I am sure I don't see—"

"Yes, you do, my dear," thought Roland; "you think he was jealous, and you are wrong; but it is good for us that you should." And in memory of the little compliment her speech had unintentionally conveyed he gave another twist to his mustache.

The outer door closed with a jar that reached him where he sat. "Thank God!" he muttered; and divining that if he now went away the girl would regret his departure, after another word or two, and despite the protestation of her manner, he bade her good-night.

It is one of the charms of our lovely climate that the temperature can fall twenty degrees in as many minutes. When Roland entered the Dunellen house he left spring in the street; when he came out again there was snow. Across the way a lamp flickered, beneath it a man was standing, from beyond came a faint noise of passing wheels, but the chance of rescue by cab or hansom was too remote for anyone but a foreigner to entertain. Roland had omitted to provide himself with any protection against a storm, yet that omission affected him but little. He had too many things to think of to be anxious about his hat; and, his hands in his pocket, his head lowered, he descended the steps, prepared to let the snow do its worst.

As he reached the pavement the man at the lamp-post crossed the street.

"Mistrial," he called, for Roland was hurrying on—"Mistrial, I want a word with you."

In a moment he was at his side, and simultaneously Roland recognized the cousin. He was buttoned up in a loose coat faced with fur, and over his head he held an umbrella. He seemed a little out of breath.

"If," he began at once, "if I hear that you ever presume to so much as speak to Miss Dunellen again, I will break every bone in your body."

The voice in which he made this threat was gruff and aggressive. As he delivered it, he closed his umbrella and swung it like a club.

"A nous deux, maintenant," mused Roland.

"And not only that—if you ever dare to enter that house again I will expose you."

"Oh, will you, though?" answered Roland. The tone he assumed was affectedly civil. "Well now, my fat friend, let me tell you this: I intend to enter that house, as you call it, to-morrow at precisely five o'clock. Let me pick you up on the way, and we can go together."

"Roland Mistrial, as sure as there is a God in heaven I will have you in the Tombs."

"See here, put up your umbrella. You are not in a condition to expose yourself—let alone anyone else. You are daft, Thorold—that is what is the matter with you. If you persist in chattering Tombs at me in a snow-storm I will answer Bloomingdale to you. You frightened me once, I admit; but I am ten years older now, and ten years less easily scared. Besides, what drivel you talk! You haven't that much to go on."

As Roland spoke his accent changed from affected suavity to open scorn. "Now stop your bluster," he continued, "and listen to me. Because you happen to find me in there, you think I have intentions on the heiress—"

"It's a lie! She—"

"There, don't be abusive. I know you want her for yourself, and I hope you get her. But please don't think that I mean to stand in your way."

"I should say not."

"In the first place, I went there on business."

"What business, I would like to know?"

"So you shall. I took some papers for Mr. Dunellen to examine—papers relative to my father's estate. To-morrow I return to learn his opinion. Next week I go abroad again. When I leave I promise you shall find your cousin still heart-whole and fancy-free."

As Roland delivered this little stab he paused a moment to note the effect. But apparently it had passed unnoticed—Thorold seemingly was engrossed in the statements that preceded it. The scowl was still on his face, but it was a scowl into which perplexity had entered, and which in entering had modified the aggressiveness that had first been there. At the moment his eyes wandered, and Roland, who was watching him, felt that he had scored a point.

"You say you are going abroad?" he said, at last.

"Yes; I have to join my wife."

At this announcement Thorold looked up at him and then down at the umbrella. Presently, with an abrupt gesture, he unfurled it and raised it above his head. As he did so, Roland smiled. For that night at least the danger had gone. Of the morrow, however, he was unassured.

"Suppose we walk along," he said, encouragingly; and before Thorold knew it, he was sharing that umbrella with his foe. "Yes," he continued, "my poor father left his affairs in a muddle, but Mr. Dunellen says he thinks he can straighten them out. You can understand that if any inkling of this thing were to reach him he would return the papers at once. You can understand that, can't you? After all, you must know that I have suffered."

"Suffered!" Thorold cried. "What's that to me? It made my mother insane."

"God knows I nearly lost my reason too. I can understand how you feel toward me: it is only what I deserve. Yet though you cannot forget, at least it can do you no good to rake this matter up."

"It is because of—" and for a second the cousin halted in his speech.

"Voilà!" mused Roland. "Je te vois venir."

"However, if you are going abroad—"

"Most certainly I am. I never expect to see Miss Dunellen again."

"In that case I will say nothing."

They had reached Fifth Avenue, and for a moment both loitered on the curb. Thorold seemed to have something to add, but he must have had difficulty in expressing it, for he nodded as though to reiterate the promise.

"I can rely upon you then, can I?" Roland asked.

"Keep out of my way, sir, and I will try, as I have tried, to forget."

A 'bus was passing, he hailed it, and disappeared.

Roland watched the conveyance, and shook the snow-flakes from his coat. "Try, and be damned," he muttered. "I haven't done with you yet."

The disdain of a revenge at hand is accounted the uniquest possible vengeance. And it is quite possible that had Roland's monetary affairs been in a better condition, on a sound and solid basis, let us say, he would willingly have put that paradox into action. But on leaving Tuxedo he happened to be extremely hungry—hungry, first and foremost, for the possession of that wealth which in this admirably conducted country of ours lifts a man above the law, and, an adroit combination of scoundrelism and incompetence aiding, sometimes lands him high among the executives of state. By political ambition, however, it is only just to say he was uninspired. In certain assemblies he had taken the trouble to assert that our government is one at which Abyssinia might sneer, but the rôle of reformer was not one which he had any inclination to attempt. Several of his progenitors figured, and prominently too, in abridgments of history; and, if posterity were not satisfied with that, he had a very clear idea as to what posterity might do. In so far as he was personally concerned, the prominence alluded to was a thing which he accepted as a matter of course: it was an integral part of himself; he would have missed it as he would have missed a leg or the point of his nose; but otherwise it left his pulse unstirred. No, his hunger was not for preferment or place. It was for the ten million which the Hon. Paul Dunellen had gathered together, and which the laws of gravitation would prevent him from carrying away when he died. That was the nature of Roland Mistrial's hunger, and as incidental thereto was the thirst to adjust an outstanding account.

Whatever the nature of that account may have been, in a more ordinary case it might have become outlawed through sheer lapse of time. But during that lapse of time Roland had been in exile because of it; and though even now he might have been willing to let it drift back into the past where it belonged, yet when the representative of it not only loomed between him and the millions, but was even attempting to gather them in for himself, the possibility of retaliation was too complete to suffer disdain. The injury, it is true, was one of his own doing. But, curiously enough, when a man injures another the more wanton that injury is the less it incites to repentance. In certain dispositions it becomes a source of malignant hate. Deserve a man's gratitude, and he may forgive you; but let him do you a wrong, and you have an enemy for life. Such is the human heart—or such at least was Roland Mistrial's.

And now, as the conveyance rumbled off into the night, he shook the snow-flakes from his coat.

"Try, and be damned," he repeated; "I haven't done with you yet."

IV.

To the New Yorker March is the vilest month of all the year. In the South it is usually serene. Mrs. Metuchen, who gave herself the airs of an invalid, and who possessed the invalid's dislike of vile weather, was aware of this; and while the first false promises of February were being protested she succeeded in persuading Miss Dunellen to accompany her out of snow-drifts into the sun. It was Aiken that she chose as refuge; and when the two ladies arrived there they felt satisfied that their choice had been a proper one—a satisfaction which they did not share alone, for a few days after their arrival Roland Mistrial arrived there too.

During the intervening weeks he had seemed idle; but it is the thinker's characteristic to appear unoccupied when he is most busily engaged, and Roland, outwardly inactive, had in reality made the most of his time.

On the morning succeeding the encounter with Thorold something kept coming and whispering that he had undertaken a task which was beyond his strength. To many of us night is apt to be more confident than are the earlier hours of the day, and the courage which Roland had exhibited spent itself and went. It is hard to feel the flutter of a bird beneath one's fingers, and, just when the fingers tighten, to discover that the bird is no longer there. Such a thing is disappointing, and the peculiarity of a disappointment consists in this—the victim of it is apt to question the validity of his own intuitions. Thus far—up to the looming of Thorold—everything had been in Roland's favor. Without appreciable effort he had achieved the impossible. In three days he had run an heiress to earth, gained her father's liking, captivated her chaperon, and, at the moment when the air was sentient with success, the highway on which he strode became suddenly tortuous and obscure. Do what he might he could not discern so much as a sign-post; and as in perplexity he twirled his thumbs, little by little he understood that he must either turn back and hunt another quarry, or stand where he was and wait. Another step on that narrowing road and he might tumble into a gully. Did he keep his word with Thorold he felt sure that Thorold would keep his word with him. But did he break it, and Thorold learn he had done so, several consequences were certain to ensue, and among them he could hear from where he stood the bang with which Mr. Dunellen's door would close. The only plank which drifted his way threatened to break into bits. He needed no one to tell him that Justine was not a girl to receive him or anyone else in the dark; and even fortune favoring, if in chance meetings he were able to fan her spark of interest for him into flame, those chance meetings would be mentioned by her to whomsoever they might concern. No, that plank was rotten; and yet in considering it, and in considering too the possibilities to which, were it a trifle stronger, it might serve as bridge, he passed that morning, a number of subsequent mornings. A month elapsed, and still he eyed that plank.

Meanwhile he had seen Miss Dunellen but once. She happened to be driving up the Avenue, but he had passed her unobserved. Then the weather became abominable, and he knew it was useless to look for her in the Park; and once he had visited her father's office and learned again, what he already knew, that in regard to the lost estate, eternity aiding, something might be recovered, but that the chances were vague as was it. And so February came and found his hunger unappeased. The alternate course which had suggested itself came back, and he determined to turn and hunt another quarry. During his sojourn abroad he had generally managed a team of three. There was the gerundive, as he termed the hindmost—the woman he was about to leave; there was another into whose graces he had entered; and there was a third in training for future use. This custom he had found most serviceable. Whatever might happen in less regulated establishments, his stable was full. And that custom, which had stood him in good stead abroad, had nothing in it to prevent adoption here. Indeed, he told himself it was because of his negligence in that particular that he found himself where he was. Instead of centring his attention on Miss Dunellen, it would have been far better to wander in and out of the glittering precincts of Fifth Avenue, and see what else he could find. After all, there was nothing like being properly provisioned. If one comestible ran short, there should be another to take its place. Moreover, if, as Jones had intimated, there were heiresses enough for export purposes, there must surely be enough to supply the home demand.

The alternate course alluded to he had therefore determined to adopt, when an incident occurred which materially altered his plans. One particularly detestable morning he read in public print that Mrs. Metuchen and Miss Dunellen were numbered among the visitors to South Carolina, and thereupon he proceeded to pack his valise. A few days later he was in Aiken, and on the forenoon of the third day succeeding his arrival, as he strolled down the verandah of the Mountain Glen Hotel, he felt at peace with the world and with himself.

It was a superb morning, half summer, half spring. In the distance a forest stretched indefinitely and lost itself in the haze of the horizon beyond. The sky was tenderly blue, and, beneath, a lawn green as the baize on a roulette-table was circled by a bright-red road. He had breakfasted infamously on food that might have been cooked by a butcher to whom breakfast is an odious thing. Yet its iniquity he accepted as a matter of course. He knew, as we all do, that for bad food, bad service, and for futility of complaint our country hotels are unrivalled, even in Spain. He was there not to enjoy himself, still less for the pleasures a blue ribbon can cause: he was there to fan into flame the interest which Miss Dunellen had exhibited; and as he strolled down the verandah, a crop under his arm, his trousers strapped, he had no intention of quarrelling with the fare. Quite a number of people were basking in the sunlight, and, as he passed, some of them turned and looked; for at Aiken men that have more than one lung are in demand, and, when Roland registered his historic name, to the unattached females a little flutter of anticipation came.

But Roland was not in search of flirtations: he moved by one group into another until he reached a corner of the verandah in which Mrs. Metuchen and

Miss Dunellen sat. Merely by the expression on the faces of those whom he greeted it was patent to the others that the trio were on familiar terms; and when presently he accompanied Miss Dunellen off the verandah, aided her to mount a horse that waited there, mounted another himself, and cantered off with the girl, the unattached females declared that the twain must be engaged. In that they were in error. As yet Roland had not said a word to the charge he might not have said to the matron. Both of these ladies had been surprised when he reached Aiken, and both had been pleased as well. In that surprise, in that pleasure, Roland had actively collaborated; and taking on himself to answer before it was framed the question which his advent naturally prompted, he stated that in journeying from Savannah to Asheville he had stopped over at Aiken as at a halfway house, and that, too, without an idea of encountering anyone whom he knew. Thereafter for several days he managed to make himself indispensable to the matron, companionable to her charge; but now, on this particular morning, as he rattled down the red road, the courage which had deserted him returned; and a few hours later, when before a mirror in his bedroom he stood arranging his cravat, he caught a reflection of Hyperion, son-in-law of Crœsus.

V.

In a fortnight that reflection was framed with a promise. Justine had put her hand in his. The threads by which he succeeded in binding her to him are needless to describe. He understood that prime secret in the art of coercing affection which consists in making one's self desired. He was never inopportune. Moreover, he saw that Justine, accustomed to the devotion of other men, accepted such devotion as a matter of course; in consequence he took another tack, and bullied her—a treatment which was new to her, and, being new, attractive. He found fault with her openly, criticised the manner in which she sat her horse, contradicted her whenever the opportunity came, and jeered—civilly, it is true, but the jeer was there and all the sharper because it was blunted—at any enthusiasm she chanced to express. And then, when she expected it least, he would be enthusiastic himself, and enthusiastic over nothing at all—some mythical deed canned in history, the beauty of a child, or the flush of the arbutus which they gathered on their rides. To others whom he encountered in her presence he showed himself so self-abnegatory, so readily pleased, sweet-tempered, and indulgent, so studious even of their susceptibilities and appreciative of what they liked and what they did not, that in comparing his manner to her and his manner to them the girl grew vexed, and one evening she told him so.

They happened to be sitting alone in a corner of the verandah. From within came the rhythm of a waltz; some dance was in progress, affectioned by the few; Mrs. Metuchen was discussing family trees with a party of Philadelphians; the air was sweet with the scent of pines and of jasmines; just above and beyond, a star was circumflexed by the moon.

"I am sorry if I have offended," he made answer to her complaint. "Do you mind if I smoke?" Without waiting for her consent he drew out a cigarette and lighted it. "I have not intended to," he added. "To-morrow I will go."

"But why? You like it here. You told me so to-day."

With a fillip of forefinger and thumb Roland tossed the cigarette out into the road. "Because I admire you," he answered curtly.

"I am glad of that."

The reproof, if reproof there were, was not in her speech, but in her voice. She spoke as one does whose due is conceded only after an effort. And for a while both were mute.

"Come, children, it is time to go to bed." Mrs. Metuchen in her fantastic fashion was hailing them from the door. Already the waltz had ceased, and as Mrs. Metuchen spoke, Justine rose from her seat.

"Good-night, Don Quichotte," the old lady added; and as the girl approached she continued in an audible undertone, "I call him Don Quichotte because he looks like the Chevalier Bayard."

"Good-night, Mrs. Metuchen, and the pleasantest of dreams." But the matron, with a wave of her glove, had disappeared, and Justine returned.

"At least you will not go until the afternoon?"

"Since you wish it, I will not."

She had stretched out her hand, but Roland, affecting not to notice it, raised his hat and turned away. Presently, and although, in spite of many a vice, he was little given to drink, he found himself at the bar superintending the blending of gin, of lemon-peel, and of soda; and as he swallowed it and put the goblet down he seemed so satisfied that the barkeeper, with the affectionate familiarity of his class, nodded and smiled.

"It takes a Remsen Cooler to do the trick, don't it?" he said.

And Roland, assenting remotely, left the bar and sought his room.

The next morning, as through different groups he sought for matron and for maid, he had a crop under his arm and in his hand a paper.

"I have been settling my bill," he announced.

"But are you going?" exclaimed Mrs. Metuchen.

"I can hardly take up a permanent residence here, can I?" he replied.

"Oh, Justine," the old lady cried, and clutched the girl by the arm, "persuade him not to." And fixing him with her glittering eyes, she added, "If you go, sir, you leave an Aiken void."

The jest passed him unnoticed. He felt that something had been said which called for applause, for Mrs. Metuchen was laughing immoderately. But his eyes were in Justine's as were hers in his.

"You will ride, will you not? I see you have your habit on." And with that, Justine assenting, he led her down the steps and aided her to the saddle.

There are numberless tentative things in life, and among them an amble through green, deserted lanes, where only birds and flowers are, has witcheries of its own. However perturbed the spirit may have been, there is that in the glow of the morning and the gait of a horse that can make it wholly serene. The traveller from Sicily will, if you let him, tell of hours so fair that even the bandits are coerced. Man cannot always be centred in self; and when to the influence of nature is added the companionship of one whose presence allures, the charm is complete. And Roland, to whom such things hitherto had been as accessories, this morning felt their spell. The roomy squalor of the village had been passed long since. They had entered a road where the trees arched and nearly hid the sky, but through the branches an eager sunlight found its way. Now and then in a clearing they would happen on some shabby, silent house, the garden gay with the tender pink of blossoming peach; and at times, from behind a log or straight from the earth, a diminutive negro would start like a kobold in a dream and offer, in an abashed, uncertain way, a bunch of white violets in exchange for coin. And once an old man, trudging along, saluted them with a fine parabola of hat and hand; and once they encountered a slatternly negress, very fat and pompous, seated behind a donkey she could have carried in her arms. But practically the road was deserted, fragrant, and still.

And now, as they rode on, interchanging only haphazard remarks, Roland swung himself from his horse, and, plucking a spray of arbutus, handed it to the girl.

"Take it," he said; "it is all I have."

His horse had wandered on a step and was nibbing at the grass, and, as he stood looking up at her, for the first time it occurred to him that she was fair. However a girl may seem in a ball-room, if she ever looks well she looks best in the saddle; and Justine, in spite of his criticism, did not sit her horse badly. Her gray habit, the high white collar and open vest, brought out the snuff-color of her eyes and hair. Her cheeks, too, this morning must have recovered some of the flush they had lost, or else the sun had been using its palette, for in them was the hue of the flower he had gathered and held.

She took it and inserted the stem in the lapel of her coat.

"Are you going?" she asked.

"What would you think of me if I remained?"

"What would I? I would think—"

As she hesitated she turned. He could see now it was not the sun alone that had been at work upon her face.

"Let me tell. You would think that a man with two arms for sole income has no right to linger in the neighborhood of a girl such as you. That is what you would think, what anyone would think; and while I care little enough about the existence which I lead in the minds of other people, yet I do care for your esteem. If I stay, I lose it. I should lose, too, my own; let me keep them both and go."

"I do not yet see why?"

"You don't!" The answer was so abrupt in tone that you would have said he was irritated at her remark, judging it unnecessary and ill-timed. "You don't!" he repeated. "Go back a bit, and perhaps you will remember that after I saw you at your house I did not come back again."

"I do indeed remember."

"The next day I saw you in the Park; I was careful not to return."

"But what have I done? You said last night—"

"Why do you question? You know it is because I love you."

"Then you shall not go."

"I must."

"You shall not, I say."

"And I shall take with me the knowledge that the one woman I have loved is the one woman I have been forced to leave."

"Roland Mistrial, how can you bear the name you do and yet be so unjust? If you leave me now it is because you care more for yourself than you ever could for me. It is not on my account you go: it is because you fear the world. There were heroes once that faced it."

"Yes, and there were Circes then, as now."

As he made that trite reply his face relaxed, and into it came an expression of such abandonment that the girl could see the day was won.

"Tell me—you will not go?"

Roland caught her hand in his, and, drawing back the gauntlet of kid, he kissed her on the wrist. "I will never leave you now," he answered; "Only promise you will not regret."

"Regret!" She smiled at the speech—or was it a smile? Her lips had moved, but it was as though they had done so in answer to some prompting of her soul. "Regret! Do you remember you asked me what I would think if you remained? Well, I thought, if you did, there were dreams which do come true."

At this avowal she was so radiant yet so troubled that Roland detained her hand. "She really loves," he mused; "and so do I." And it may be, the forest aiding, that, in the answering pressure which he gave, such heart as he had went out and mingled with her own.

"Between us now," he murmured, "it is for all of time."

"Roland, how I waited for you!"

Again her lips moved and she seemed to smile, but now her eyes were no longer in his, they were fixed on some vista visible only to herself. She looked rapt, but she looked startled as well. When a girl first stands face to face with love it allures and it frightens too.

Roland dropped her hand; he caught his horse and mounted it. In a moment he was at her side again.

"Justine!"

And the girl turning to him let her fresh lips meet and rest upon his own. Slowly he disengaged the arm with which he had steadied himself on her waist.

"If I lose you now—" he began.

"There can be no question of losing," she interrupted. "Have we not come into our own?"

"But others may dispute our right. There is your cousin, to whom I thought you were engaged; and there is your father."

"Oh, as for Guy—" and she made a gesture. "Father, it is true, may object; but let him. I am satisfied; in the end he will be satisfied also. Why, only the other day I wrote him you were here."

"H'm!" At the intelligence he wheeled abruptly.

Already Justine had turned, and lowering her crop she gave her horse a little tap. The beast was willing enough; in a moment the two were on a run, and as Roland's horse, a broncho, by-the-way, one of those eager animals that decline to remain behind, rushed forward and took the lead, "Remember!" she cried, "you are not to leave me now."

But the broncho was self-willed, and this injunction Roland found or pretended it difficult to obey; and together, through the green lane and out of it, by long, dismal fields of rice, into the roomy squalor of the village and on to the hotel, they flew as though some fate pursued. Justine never forgot that ride, nor did Roland either.

At the verandah steps Mrs. Metuchen was in waiting. "I have a telegram from your father," she called to Justine. "He wishes you to return to-morrow."

"To-morrow?" the girl exclaimed.

"Thorold has learned I am here, and has told," her lover reflected. And swinging from his saddle he aided the girl to alight.

"To-morrow," Mrs. Metuchen with large assumption of resignation replied; "and we may be thankful he did not say to-day."

And as Roland listened to the varying interpretations of the summons which, during the absence of her charge, Mrs. Metuchen's riotous imagination had found time to conceive, "Thorold has told," he repeated to himself, "but he has told too late."

After a morning such as that, an afternoon on a piazza is apt to drag. Of this Roland was conscious. Moreover, he had become aware that his opportunities were now narrowly limited; and presently, as Mrs. Metuchen's imaginings subsided and ceased, he asked the girl whether, when dinner was over, she would care to take a drive.

Protest who may, at heart every woman is a match-maker; and Mrs. Metuchen was not an exception. In addition to this, she liked family-trees, she was in cordial sympathy with good-breeding, and Roland, who possessed both, had, through attentions which women of her age appreciate most, succeeded in detaining her regard. In conversation, whenever Justine happened to be mentioned, she had a habit of extolling that young woman—not beyond her deserts, it is true, but with the attitude of one aware that the girl had done something which she ought to be ashamed of, yet to which no one was permitted to allude. This attitude was due to the fact that she suspected her, and suspected that everyone else suspected her, of an attachment for her cousin Guy. Now Guy Thorold had never appealed to Mrs. Metuchen. He was not prompt with a chair; when she unrolled her little spangle of resonant names he displayed no eagerness in face or look. Such things affect a woman. They ruffle her flounces and belittle her in her own esteem. As a consequence, she disliked Guy Thorold; from the heights of that dislike she was even wont to describe him as Poke—a word she could not have defined had she tried, but which suggested to her all the attributes of that which is stupid and under-bred. Roland, on the other hand, seemed to her the embodiment of just those things which Thorold lacked, and in the hope that he might cut the cousin out she extolled him to her charge in indirect and subtle ways. You young men who read this page mind you of this: if you would succeed in love or war, be considerate of women who are no longer young. They ask but an attention, a moment of your bountiful days, some little act of deference, and in exchange they sound your praises more deftly than ever trumpeter or beat of drums could do.

But because Mrs. Metuchen had an axe of her own to grind was not to her mind a reason why she should countenance a disregard of the Satanic pomps of that which the Western press terms Etiquette. And so it happened that, when Roland asked Justine whether she would care to drive, before the girl could answer, the matron stuck her oar in:

"Surely, Mr. Mistrial, you cannot think Miss Dunellen could go with you alone. Not that I see any impropriety in her doing so, but there is the world."

The world at that moment consisted of a handful of sturdy consumptives impatiently waiting the opening of the dining-room doors. And as Roland considered that world, he mentally explored the stable.

"Of course not," he answered; "if Miss Dunellen cares to go, I will have a dogcart and a groom."

With that sacrifice to conventionality Mrs. Metuchen was content. For Justine to ride unchaperoned was one thing, but driving was another matter. And later on, in the cool of the afternoon, as Roland bowled the girl over the yielding sand, straight to the sunset beyond, he began again on the duo which they had already rehearsed, and when Justine called his attention to the groom, he laughed a little, and well he might. "Don't mind him," he murmured; "he is deaf."

In earlier conversations he had rarely spoken of himself, and, when he had, it had been in that remote fashion which leaves the personal pronoun at the door. There is nothing better qualified to weary the indifferent than the speech in which the I jumps out; and knowing this, he knew too that that very self-effacement before one whose interest is aroused excites that interest to still higher degrees. The Moi seul est haïssable is an old maxim, one that we apprehend more or less to our cost no doubt, and after many a sin of egotism; but when it is learned by rote, few others serve us in better stead. In Roland's relations with Justine thus far it had served him well. It had filled her mind with questions which she did not feel she had the right to ask, and in so filling it had occupied her thoughts with him. It was through arts of this kind that Machiavelli earned his fame.

But at present circumstances had changed. She had placed her hand in his; she had avowed her love. The I could now appear; its welcome was assured. And as they drove along the sand-hills she told him of herself, and drew out confidences in exchange. And such confidences! Had the groom not been deaf they might have given him food for thought. But they must have satisfied Justine, for when they reached the hotel again her eyes were so full of meaning that, had Mrs. Metuchen met her in a pantry instead of on the verandah, she could have seen unspectacled that the girl was fairly intoxicated —drunk with that headiest cup of love which is brewed not by the contact of two epiderms, but through communion of spirit and unison of heart.

That evening, when supper was done, Mrs. Metuchen, to whom any breath of night was synonymous with miasmas and microbes, settled herself in the parlor, and in the company of her friends from School Lane discussed that inexhaustible topic—Who Was and Who Was Not.

But the verandah, deserted at this hour by the consumptives, had attractions for Justine, for Roland as well; and presently, in a corner of it that leaned to the south, both were seated, and, at the moment, both were dumb. On the horizon, vague now and undiscerned, the peach-blossoms and ochres of sunset had long since disappeared; but from above rained down the light and messages of other worlds; the sky was populous with stars that seemed larger and nearer than they do in the north; Venus in particular shone like a neighborly sun that had strayed afar, and in pursuit of her was a moon, a new one, so slender and yellow you would have said, a feather that a breath might blow away. In the air were the same inviting odors, the scent of heliotrope and of violets, the invocations of the woodlands, the whispers of the pines. The musicians had been hushed, or else dismissed, for no sound came from them that night.

Roland had not sought the feverish night to squander it in contemplation. His hand moved and caught Justine's. It resisted a little, then lay docile in his own. For she was new to love. Like every other girl that has passed into the twenties, she had a romance in her life, two perhaps, but romances immaterial as children's dreams, and from which she had awaked surprised, noting the rhythm yet seeking the reason in vain. They had passed from her as fancies do; and, just as she was settling down into leisurely acceptance of her cousin, Roland had appeared, and when she saw him a bird within her burst into song, and she knew that all her life she had awaited his approach. To her he was the fabulous prince that arouses the sleeper to the truth, to the meaning, of love. He had brought with him new currents, wider vistas, and horizons solid and real. He differed so from other men that her mind was pleasured with the thought he had descended from a larger sphere. She idealized him as girls untrained in life will do. He was the lover unawaited yet not wholly undivined, tender-hearted, impeccable, magnificent, incapable of wrong—the lover of whom she may never have dreamed, yet who at last had come. And into his keeping she gave her heart, and was glad, regretting only it was not more to give. She had no fears; her confidence was assured as Might, and had you or I or any other logician passed that way and demonstrated as clearly as a = a that she was imbecile in her love, she would not have thanked either of us for our pains. When a woman loves—and whatever the cynic may affirm, civilization has made her monandrous—she differs from man in this: she gives either the first-fruits of her affection, or else the semblance of an after-growth. There are men, there are husbands and lovers even, who will accept that after-growth and regard it as the verdure of an enduring spring. But who, save a lover, is ever as stupid as a husband? Man, on the other hand, is constant never. Civilization has not improved him in the least. And when on his honor he swears he has never loved before, his honor goes unscathed, for he may never yet have loved a woman as he loves the one to whom he swears.

With Justine this was the primal verdure. Had she not met Roland Mistrial, she might, and in all probability would, have exhibited constancy in affection, but love would have been uncomprehended still. As it was, she had come into her own; she was confident in it and secure; and now, though by nature she was rebellious enough, as he caught her hand her being went out to him, and as it went it thrilled.

"I love you," he said; and his voice was so flexible that it would have been difficult to deny that he really did. "I will love you always, my whole life through."

The words caressed her so well she could have pointed to the sky and repeated with Dona Sol:

"Regarde: plus de feux, plus de bruit. Tout se tait.La lune tout à l'heure à l'horizon montait:Tandis que tu parlais, sa lumière qui trembleEt ta voix, toutes deux m'allaient au cœur ensemble:Je me sentais joyeuse et calme, ô mon amant!Et j'aurais bien voulu mourir en ce moment."

But at once some premonition seemed to visit her. "Roland," she murmured, "what if we leave our happiness here?"

And Roland, bending toward her, whispered sagely: "We shall know then where to find it."

VI.

New York meanwhile, in its effeminateness, had forgotten the snow, and was listening to the sun. And the day after the return from Aiken, as Roland, in accordance with an agreement of which the locus sigilli had a kiss for token, went down to knock at Mr. Dunellen's office door, the sky was as fair as it had been in the South. Yet to him it was unobtrusive. His mind was occupied with fancies that had a birth, a little span of life, and which in passing away were succeeded by others as ephemeral as themselves—thoughts about nothing at all that came and went unnoticed: a man he had met in Corfu, and whom a face in the street recalled; the glisten of silk in a window that took him back to Japan;—but beneath them was a purpose settled and dominant, a resolution to trick Fate and outwit it—one which, during the journey from Aiken, had so possessed him that, in attending to the wants of Mrs. Metuchen or in ministering to Justine, at times he had been quasi-somnambulistic, at others wholly vague. But now, as he gave his card to an office-boy, to all outward intent he was confident and at ease; he picked up a paper and affected to lose himself in its columns. Presently the boy returned, and he was ushered into the room which he had previously visited. On this occasion Mr. Dunellen was not seated, but standing, his back to the door. As Roland entered he turned, and the young man stepped forward, his hand outstretched.

To his contentment, and a little also to his surprise, in answer to that outstretched hand Honest Paul extended his, and Roland had the pleasure of holding three apparently docile fingers in his own; but in a moment they withdrew themselves, and he felt called upon to speak.

"Mr. Dunellen," he began, with that confident air a creditor has who comes to claim his due, "Mr. Dunellen, I have ventured to interrupt you again. And again I am a suppliant. But this time it is of your daughter, not of my father, that—"

He hesitated, and well he might. Mr. Dunellen, who had remained standing, and who in so doing had prevented Roland from sitting down, now assumed the suspicious appearance of one who detects an unpleasant smell; his features contracted, and for no other reason, apparently, than that of intimidating the suppliant in his prayer.

But Roland was not to be abashed; he recovered himself, and continued glibly enough: "The matter is this. I am sincerely attached to your daughter, and I am come to ask your consent to our marriage."

"That is the purpose of your visit, is it?"

"It is."

"My daughter is aware of it, I suppose?"

"She is."

"And she consented, did she?"

"Perfectly."

"H'm! My daughter has made a mistake. I told her as much last night. There can be no question of marriage. You will do me the favor to let the matter drop."

"I am hot a rich man, Mr. Dunellen, but—"

"So I am informed. But that has nothing to do with it. There are other things that I take into consideration, and in view of them I insist that this matter be dropped."

"Mr. Dunellen, I love your daughter; I have reason to believe that she cares for me. We became engaged a few days ago. I came here now to ask your consent. If you refuse it, I have at least the right to ask what your objection is."

"Rather unnecessary, don't you think?"

"I cannot imagine, sir, what you mean." And Roland, holding himself unaffectedly straight, without the symptom of a pose, looked the old man in the eyes.

That look Mr. Dunellen returned. "Take a seat," he said; and, motioning Roland to a chair, he sat down himself.

"All this is needless," he announced; "but since you are anxious for an explanation, I will give it. In the first place, when you were at my house you remember that my nephew Dr. Thorold happened in. The other day I mentioned to him that you were at Aiken. He then informed me of a certain incident in your career, one which you have not forgotten, and of which I do not care to speak. I may say, however, that it utterly precludes the possibility of any further intercourse between my daughter and yourself."

And the old man, still gazing at his guest, added: "This explanation should, it seems to me, suffice." But he made no attempt to rise, or to signify that the interview was at an end, and Roland, who was shrewd, interpreted this in his own favor. "He is not altogether positive," he reflected, "but he can be so to-morrow," and with a show of shame that did him credit he hung his head.

"I had thought the incident to which you refer was forgotten," he murmured, penitently enough.

"Forgotten? Do you suppose Thorold forgets? Do you suppose any man could forget a thing like that—a sister's death, a mother's insanity? No, you did not think it was forgotten. What you thought was this: you thought that my nephew would hesitate to speak; and indeed even to me for ten years he has kept silent. But now—there, you need not fear a criminal charge. It was that you feared once, I understand, and it was on that account you went abroad. At this date, of course, no proof is possible; and, even were it otherwise, a charge would not be brought. Linen of that kind is better washed at home."

"Mr. Dunellen, if you could know! It is the regret of my life."

"That I can believe; but I believe also that our natures never vary. We may mould and shape them to our uses, but beneath the surface they remain unchanged. I say this parenthetically. In regard to this incident there are in one particular certain excuses you might allege—youth for instance, inexperience, common attraction, love even. If you did, I could enter into them. I have been young myself, and I have no wish to imply that through the temptations of youth I passed unscathed. The man who asserts he has reminds me of the horseman who declares he has never been thrown. Nor because your victim happened to be my niece am I actuated by retrospective indignation. I am too old for that; and, moreover, the incident is too stale. No: my reason for forbidding my daughter to receive you, as I have done, is this: the man that can seduce a girl, and then, to conceal the effect, permit her to be butchered by a quack, especially when he could have protected her by marriage—that man, Mr. Mistrial, I tell you very plainly, is a scoundrel, and being a scoundrel will never be anything else." And as Honest Paul made this assertion he stood up and nodded affirmatively at his guest.

"You are very hard, Mr. Dunellen."

"I may be, but so is justice."

"If I could tell you all. It was so sudden, so unpremeditated even, at the first idea of a possibility of a catastrophe I lost my head."

"It was your honor you lost."

"Yes, and for years I have tried to recover it."

"That I am glad to learn, and I hope you have succeeded; but—"

"And will you not aid me?"

"In my sight you can never appear an honest man."

At this reproach, Roland, who had sat like Abjection, one hand supporting his head, his eyes lowered and his body bent, sprang to his feet.

"There are several forms of honesty," he exclaimed, "and frankness I believe is counted among them. That you evidently possess. Let me emulate you in it. I intend that your daughter shall be my wife. If you don't care to come to the wedding your presence can be dispensed with." And without any show of anger, but with an inclination of the head that was insolent in its deference, he picked up his hat and left the room.

Presently he found himself in the street. "Who is ever as stupid as a wise man?" he queried, and laughed a little to himself—"unless"—and he fell to wondering whether Dunellen could have told his daughter all. On the corner a cab was loitering; he hailed and entered it. A little later he was ringing at the door of Honest Paul's abode.

Yes, Miss Dunellen was at home. And as the servant drew the portière to the drawing-room aside, Roland was visited by that emotion the gambler knows who waits the turning of a card. Another second, and the expression of the girl's face would tell him what the future held. The drawing-room, however, happened to be untenanted, and as he paced its spacious splendors he still wondered was she or was she not informed. In a corner was a landscape signed Courbet—a green ravine shut down by bluest sky. The coloring was so true, it jarred. In another was a statue—a cloaked and hooded figure of Death supporting a naked girl. As he contemplated it, he heard the tinkle of the portière rings. It was she, he knew; he turned, and at once his heart gave an exultant throb; in her eyes was an invitation; he put his arms about her, and for a moment held her so.

She does not know, he told himself, and to her he murmured, "I have come to say good-bye."

"Wait, Roland." She led him to a seat. "Wait; I spoke to father last night; he has some objection—"

"I told you I was poor—"

"It is that, I suppose; he did not say—"

"He will never consent, unless—"

"There, Roland. I know him best." She closed her eyes, and as he gazed at her it seemed to him she had done so to shut some memory out. "It is money with him always; you do not know—" And between her parted lips she drew a breath he heard. "Last night he told me I must never see you again. Hitherto his will has ruled: it is my turn to-day."

With this there came a splendor to her he had never marked before; she looked defiant, and resolute as well. There was strength in her face, and beauty too.

"He is unjust," she added. "It was my duty to tell him, and there my duty ends. I am not a school-girl. I know my mind; better, perhaps, than he knows his own. I have obeyed him always. It is easy to obey, but now I will act for myself."

"He will never give his consent," Roland repeated.

"He may keep it, then."

Within her something seemed to rankle; and as Roland, mindful of the slightest change in her expression, detected this, he wondered what it could portend.

"Sweetheart," he ventured, "I have these two arms; they are all in all for you."

At this Justine awoke at once. "If I did not know it—feel it; if I were not sure of it, do you think I would speak to you as I do? No, Roland. I have something of my own; when we are married, believe me, his consent will come at once."

"It is not his consent I want—you know that; it is yours."

"You have it, Roland; I gave it you among the pines."

"Where is your hat, then? Let us go."

He caught her to him again, then suffered her to leave the room. And as the portière which he had drawn that she might pass fell back into its former folds, for a moment he stood perplexed. Somewhere a screw was loose, he could have sworn. But where? Could it be that Honest Paul was supporting a separate establishment? or did Justine think he wished to mate her to some plutocrat of his choice? The first supposition was manifestly absurd; the second troubled him so little that he turned and occupied himself with the naked girl swooning in the arms of Death.

"I am ready, Roland." It was Justine, bonneted and veiled, buttoning her glove.

"I have a cab," he answered, and followed her to the door.

VII.

When Roland and Justine re-entered the drawing-room that afternoon they found Mr. Dunellen there. With him was Guy Thorold.

During the infant days of photography family groups were so much in vogue that anyone with an old album in reach can find them there in plenty. They are faded, no doubt; the cut of the garments is absurd; even the faces seem to have that antique look which is peculiar to the miniatures of people dead and departed: yet the impression they convey is admirably exalting. That gentleman in the wonderful coat must have been magnificent in every sphere of life: his mere pose, his attitude, is convincing as a memoir. And that lady in the camel's-hair shawl—how bewitchingly lovable she surely was! There is her daughter, who might be her niece, so prettily does she seem inclined to behave; and there is the son, a trifle effaced perhaps, yet with the makings of a man manifest even in that effacement. Oh, good people! let us hope you were really as amiable as you look: the picture is all we have of you; even your names are forgot; and truly it were discomforting to have the impression you convey disturbed in its slightest suggestion. We love you best as you are; we prefer you so. I, for one, will have none of that cynicism which hints that had a snap camera caught you unprepared the charm would disappear.

Yet now, in the present instance, as Mr. Dunellen and his nephew stood facing Roland and Justine, a photographer who had happened there could have taken a family group which would in no manner have resembled those which our albums hold.

"I told you last night," Mr. Dunellen was shrieking, "that I forbade you to see that man."

And Justine, raising her veil, answered, "He was not my husband then."

"Husband!" The old man stared at his daughter, his face distorted and livid with rage. "If you—"

But whatever threat he may have intended to make, Thorold interrupted.

"He is married already," he cried; "he is no more your husband than I."

At this announcement Mr. Dunellen let an arm he had outstretched fall to his side; he turned to Thorold, and Justine looked wonderingly in Roland's face.

"What does he mean?" she asked.

Roland shrugged his shoulders, "God knows," he answered. "He must be screwed."

"You are married," Thorold called out. "You needn't attempt to deny it here."

"I don't in the least: this lady has just done me the honor to become my wife."

"But you have another—you told me so yourself."

Roland, who had been really perplexed, could not now conceal a smile. He remembered that he had indeed told Thorold he was married, but he had done so merely as an easy way of diverting the suspicions which that gentleman displayed.

Justine, still looking at him, caught the smile.

"Why don't you speak?" she asked.

"What is there to say?" he answered. "It is false as an obituary."

"Then tell him so."

But for that there was no time. Mr. Dunellen, trained in procedure, had already questioned Thorold, and found that save Mistrial's word he had nothing to grapple on.

"Leave the house, sir," he shouted, and pointed to the door.

"When he goes, father, I go too."

"Then go." And raising his arms above his head as though to invoke the testimony of heaven, he bawled at her, "I disown you."

"There's Christian forbearance," muttered Mistrial; and he might have asserted as much, but Justine had lowered her veil.

"Come," she said.

And as she and her husband passed from the room the old man roared impotently "I disinherit you—you are no longer my child."

"Didn't you tell me he had been used to having his own way?" Roland asked, as he put Justine in the cab; and without waiting for an answer he told the driver to go to the Brunswick, and took a seat at her side.

In certain crises the beauty of an old adage asserts itself even to the stupidest. Roland had taken the bull by the horns and got tossed for his pains; yet even while he was in the air he kept assuring himself that he would land on his feet. The next morning the memory of the old man's anger affected him not at all. Passion, he knew, burns itself out, and its threats subside into ashes. The relentless parent was a spectacle with which the stage had made him so familiar that he needed no prompter's book to tell him that when the curtain fell it would be on a tableau of awaited forgiveness. And even though Mr. Dunellen and the traditional father might differ, yet on the subject of wills and bequests he understood that the legislature had in its wisdom prevented a testator from devising more than one-half his property to the detriment of kith and of kin. If things came to the worst Justine would get five million instead of ten; and five million, though not elastic enough, as Jones had said, to entertain with, still represented an income that sufficed for the necessaries of life. On that score his mind was at rest. Moreover, it was manifestly impossible for Justine's father to live forever: there was an odor of fresh earth about him which to his own keen nostrils long since had betokened the grave; and if meanwhile he chose to keep the purse-strings drawn, Justine had enough from her mother's estate to last till the strings were loosed.

Rents are high in New York, and to those bred in certain of its manors there is a choice between urban palaces and suburban flats. But Paris is less fastidious. In that lovely city a thousand-franc note need not be spent in a day; and in Italy the possibilities of the lira are great.

In view of these things, Roland and his wife one week later took ship and sailed for France.

PART II.

I.

To those that have suffered certain things there are forms of entertainment which neither amuse nor bore, but which pain. And this evening, as Justine sat in the stalls, the play which was being given, and which, as plays go, was endurable enough, caused her no pleasure, no weariness even, only a longing to get away and be alone. Now and then a shudder visited her, her hand tightened on her fan, and at times she would close her eyes, dull her hearing, and try to fancy that her girlhood was recovered, that she was free again, that she was dead, that her husband was—anything imaginable in fact, save the knowledge that she was there, side-by-side with him, and that presently they would return together to the hideousness of their uptown flat.

She had been married now a little more than two years, and during the latter portion of that time life had held for her that precise dose of misery which is just insufficient to produce uncertainties of thought in a mind naturally exalted. There had indeed been moments in which the possibility of insanity had presented itself, and there had been moments also in which she would have welcomed that possibility as a grateful release: but those moments had passed, the possibility with them; and this evening as she sat in the stalls her outward appearance was much such as it had been two years before. But within, where her heart had been, was a cemetery.

Among our friends and acquaintances there are always those who to our knowledge have tombstones of their own. But there are others that evolve a world—one that glows, subsides, and dies away unknown to any save themselves. The solitudes of space appall; the solitudes of the heart can be as endless as they. In those which Justine concealed, a universe had had its being and its subsidence; a universe with gem-like hopes for stars—one in which the sun had been so eager its rays had made her blind. There had been comets gorgeous and tangential as aspirations ever are; there had been the colorless ether of which dreams are made; and for cosmic matter there was love. But now it was all dispersed; there was nothing left, one altar merely—the petrefaction of a prayer erected long since in the depths of her distress, and which for conscience' sake now and then she tended still.

And now, as the play at which she assisted unrolled before her unseeing eyes, one by one scenes from another drama rose unsummoned in its stead. First was the meeting with Mistrial at Tuxedo, then the episode at Aiken, the marriage that followed, and the banishment that ensued: a banishment, parenthetically, which at the time being she was powerless to understand. Her father's anger had indeed weighed on her; but it was not wholly that—she was too much in love to let it be more than a shadow on her delight; nor was it because of unfamiliar lands: it was that little by little, through incidents originally misunderstood and then more completely grasped, the discovery, avoided yet ever returning, came to her, stayed with her, and made her its own —that the man whom she had loved and the man whom she had married were separate and distinct.

The psychologist of woman has yet to appear, and if he keep us waiting may it not be because every woman he analyzes has a sister who differs from her? The moment he formulates a rule it is over-weighted by exceptions. Woman often varies, the old song says; but not alone in her affections does she do so: she varies in temperament as well. And, after all, is it not the temperament that makes or mars a life? Justine, in discovering that the man she married and the man whom she loved were separate and distinct, instead of being disgusted with herself and with him, as you, madam, might have been, tried her utmost to forget the lover and love the husband that had come in his place. In this effort she had pride for an aid. The humiliation which the knowledge of self-deception brings is great, but when that knowledge becomes common property the humiliation is increased. The world—not the world that ought to be, but the world as it is—is more apt to smile than condole. There may be much joy in heaven over the sinner that repents: on earth the joy is at his downfall. And according to the canons we have made for ourselves, Justine, in listening to the dictates of her heart instead of to those of her father, had sinned, so grievously even that that father had bid her begone from his sight. She was aware of this, and in consequence felt it needful to hold her head the higher. And so for a while she made pride serve as fig-leaf to her nakedness. If abashed at heart, at least the world should be uninformed of that abashment.

This effort on her part Mistrial hindered to the best of his ability. Whether or not he loved her, whether save himself he was capable of loving anyone, who shall say? Men too are difficult to decipher. There were hours when after some écart he would come to her so penitent, so pleasant to the eye, and seemingly so afflicted at his own misconduct, that Justine found the strength—or the weakness, was it?—to forgive and to forget anew.

During this period they lived not sumptuously, perhaps, but in that large and liberal fashion which requires a ponderable rent-roll to support; and at that time, however Mistrial comported himself elsewhere, in her presence he had the decency to seem considerate, and affectionate as well. But meanwhile, through constant demands, the value of the letter of credit into which he had converted the better part of her mother's estate became impaired. Retrenchment was necessary, and that is never a pleasant thing. The man that passes out of poverty into wealth finds the passage so easy, so Lethean even, that he is apt to forget what poverty was; but when, as sometimes happens, he is obliged to retrace his steps, he walks bare of foot through a path of thorns. To count gold, instead of strewing it, is irritating to anyone not a sage, and Mistrial, who was not a sage, was irritated; and having, a wife within beck and call he vented that irritation on her.

It was at this time that Justine began to feel the full force of the banishment. That her husband was, and in all probability would continue to be, unfaithful to her, was a matter which she ended by accepting with a degree of good sense which is more common than is generally supposed. At first she had been indeed indignant, and when in that indignation her anger developed into a heat that was white and sentiable, Mistrial experienced no remorse whatever, only a desire to applaud. He liked the force and splendor of her arraignment; it took him out of himself; it made him feel that he was appreciated—feared even;

that a word from him, and a tempest was loosened or enchained.

But what is there to which we cannot accustom ourselves? Justine ended, not by a full understanding of the fact that man is naturally polygamous; but little by little, through channels undiscerned even by herself, the idea came to her that, if the man she loved could find pleasure in the society of other women, it was because she was less attractive than they. It was this that brought her patience, the more readily even in that, at her first paroxysm, Mistrial, a trifle alarmed lest she might leave him, had caught her in his arms, and sworn in a whisper breathed in her ear, that of all the world he loved her best.

Madam, you who do the present writer the honor to read this page are convinced, he is sure, that your husband would rather his tongue cleaved to the roof of his mouth than break the vow which bound you to him. But you, madam, have married a man faithful and tried. You know very well with what dismay he tells you of Robinson's scandalous conduct, and you know also how he pities Robinson's poor little wife; yet when, in your sorrow at what that poor little woman has to put up with, you are tempted to go and condole with her, pause, madam—Mrs. Robinson may be equally tempted to condole with You.

There are—in Brooklyn, in Boston, and in other recondite regions—a number of clever people who have been brought up with the idea that Divorce was instituted for just such a thing as this. Yet in one hundred cases out of a hundred-and-one a woman who appeals to the law never does so because her husband has broken a certain commandment. If his derelictions are confined to that particular offence she may bewail, and we all bewail with her; but if she wants the sympathy of judge, of jury, and of newspaper-public too, she must be prepared to allege other grievances. She must show that her husband is unkind, that he is sarcastic, that he is given to big words and short sentences; in brief, that he has developed traits which render life in common no longer to be endured.

It was traits of this description that Mistrial unexpectedly developed, and it was during their development that the sense of banishment visited Justine. She was unable to make further transference of her affections; the lover had disappeared; the husband she had tried to love in his place had gone as well. For sole companion she had a man who had worn a mask and dropped it; where he had been considerate, he was selfish; when he spoke, it was to find fault; now that he could no longer throw her money out of the windows, he threw his amiability in its stead. By day he was taciturn, insultingly dumb; at night he was drunk.

Mistrial had served his novitiate where the pochard is rare. It is we that drink, and with us the English, the Slavs, and Teutons; but in the East and among the Latins sobriety is less a matter of habit than of instinct. And in lands where man prefers to keep his head clear, Mistrial, at that age, which is one of the most impressionable of all, had seen no reason to lose his own. But presently the small irritations of enforced economy affected his manners, and his habits as well. He took to absinthe in the morning, and, as he happened to be in France, he drank at night that brutal brandy they give you there. Not continuously, it is true. There were days when the man for whom Justine had forsaken her home returned so completely she could almost fancy he had never gone. Then, without a word of warning, at the very moment when Faith was gaining fresh foothold, the tragi-comedy would be renewed; he was off again, no one knew whither, returning only when the candle had been utterly consumed.

Such things are enough to affect any woman's patience, and Justine's became wholly warped. It was unaccountable to her that he could treat her as he did. She watched the gradual transformation of the perfect lover into the perfect beast with a species of sorrow—a dual sorrow in whose component parts there was pity for herself and for him as well.

The idea that he had married her uniquely because of her father's wealth, that he was impatient to get it, and that when he got it he would squander all he could on other women, occurred to her only in the remotest ways, and then only through some expression which, in his exasperation of the diminishing bank account and the unreasonable time which it took her father to forgive her, fell from him now and then by chance. For Mistrial had indeed counted on that forgiveness. He had even counted on receiving it by cable, of finding that it had preceded and awaited them before their ship reached France. And when, to use an idiom of that land, it made itself expected, he was confident that the longer it delayed the completer it would be. At the utmost he had not dreamed that the old man would detain it more than a few months; but when twenty-four went by, and not only no forgiveness was manifest, but through his own improvidence the funds ran low,—so low, in fact, that unless forgiveness were presently forthcoming they would be in straits indeed,—he dictated a letter, penitent and humble, one in which impending poverty stood out as clearly as though it had been engraved, and which it revolted her to send. Its inspiration, however, must have been patent to Mr. Dunellen, for that gentlemen's reply, expressed in the third person, was to the effect that if his daughter returned to him he would provide for her as he had always done, but in no other circumstances could he assist.

Had Justine been anyone but herself she might have acted on the invitation: but the tone of it hurt her; she was annoyed at having permitted herself to send the letter Mistrial had dictated, and to which this was the reply. Her pride was up—all the more surely because she knew her father had been right; and there is just this about pride—as a matter of penitence it forces us to suffer those consequences of our own wrongdoing which through a simple confession it were easy to escape. To Justine such confession was impossible. She had left her father in the full certainty that he was wrong, and when she found he was not, death to her were preferable to any admission of the grievousness of her own mistake.

At this juncture Mistrial's aunt assisted at the funeral of a sister spinster, sat in a draught, caught cold in her throat, and, the glottis enlarging, strangled one night in her bed. By her will the St. Nicholas Hospital received the bulk of her property. The rest of her estate was divided among relatives; to her nephew Roland Mistrial—3d no longer—was bequeathed the princely sum of ten thousand dollars in cash. At the news of this munificence Roland swore and grit his teeth. Had his circumstances been different it is probable that the ten thousand, together with some enduring insult, he would have flung after her to the eternal purgatory where he prayed she had gone. As it was, the modicity of the bequest sobered him. Through some impalpable logic he had counted but little on any inheritance at all; he had indeed hoped vaguely that she might die and leave him what she had; and it may even be that, had he learned that her will was in his favor, and had a suitable opportunity presented itself, in some perfectly decorous manner he would have hastened his aunt's demise. But concerning her will he had no information; moreover, during his visit to the States the old lady saw as little of him as she could help; and when she did see him, in spite of gout and the ailments of advancing years there was such a rigidity in her manner that the nephew told himself she might live long enough to see him hanged. As a consequence he had expected nothing. But when the news of her death reached him, together with the intelligence that instead of the competence he might possibly have had he was mentioned merely to the tune of ten thousand dollars,—this outrage, in conjunction with Dunellen's relentlessness, sobered him to that degree, that for a day and a night he gave himself to a debauch of thought. From this orgy he issued with clearer mind. It may be—though the idea advanced is one that can only be hazarded—it may be that had his aunt disposed of her estate in his favor he would there and then have washed his hands of the job he had undertaken, and left his wife to her own devices. As it was, he saw that, to keep his head above water, the only possible plank was one that Mr. Dunellen might send in his reach; and it was with the knowledge that before the present scanty windfall disappeared some conquest of Honest Paul's affection should be attempted that he determined to return to New York. Once there again, who knew what might happen? Surely, if the preceding year Mr. Dunellen had strength for violence, to the naked eye he was even then manifestly infirm. There was no gainsaying the matter—he at least would not live very long. As to the disposition of his property after death Mistrial was still assured. Whatever his attitude might be for the present, in the end he could not wholly disinherit Justine—at least one-half the property must come to her. On that fact Mistrial would have staked his life; after all, it was the one hope he had left; and an ultimate hope, we all know, is the thing we part with last.

Thereupon he recovered himself. He became amiable and considerate—a change of demeanor which gave Justine a chill. She consented nevertheless to the return trip, and the day after arriving called at her father's house. When she got back to the hotel where they had put up Mistrial was waiting for her. In answer to his questions she told him that her father was willing to receive her, but her alone. "You must take your choice," he had said, she repeated—"You must take your choice."

"And what is that choice?" Mistrial had asked.

"I have made it," she answered, "and by it I will abide."

But at this he had expostulated; and when, seeing at last what he meant—understanding that he would have her feign a compliance for the sake of coin which at her father's death she could come back and share with him—when, divining the infamy of his thought, she refused, he had struck her in the face.

Because a man is not Chesterfield, it does not follow he is Sykes. Mistrial had never struck a woman before, and in this initial assault it is probable that he was actuated less by a desire to punish than by that force which overmasters him who has ceased to be master of himself. By instinct he was not a gentleman; for some time past he had not even taken the trouble to appear one; yet at that moment, dancing in derision before him, he saw the letters that form the monosyllable Cad. The sense of abasement he displayed was so immediate and sincere, that Justine, who, trembling with anger and disgust, stood staring in his face, read it there and understood. Instead of separating them forever, the blow reunited their hands. During the week that followed they were nearer to each other than they had been for months before. The reconciliation was seemingly complete. Mistrial made himself the lover again, and Justine permitted herself to be wooed. They left their hotel and found a flat—a furnished apartment in the neighborhood of Central Park; and there the storm departing placed a rainbow in its stead.

A rainbow, however, is not a fixture, and this one went its way. While Justine closed her eyes Mistrial's were alert. He had no intention of suffering her to be disinherited, and though it was well enough to rely on the courts it was better still not to be forced to do so. Rather than run an avoidable risk he would have abandoned his wife, and forced her through that abandonment to return to her father's house, convinced that afterwards he could win her together with the estate back again to him. Meanwhile another interview could not in any way jeopardize the chances to which he clung. On the contrary, it might be highly serviceable. Mr. Dunellen, he had learned, was much broken; he had given up his practice, the the world even, everything in fact save perhaps the devil that was in him, and sat uncompanioned in the desolate and spacious emptiness of his house. It was only natural that he should wish to coerce his daughter into obedience; yet now that he saw she was steadfast, her pride unhumbled still, it was not improbable that he would yield; it was presumable even that he was then waiting, weak of heart, prepared at her next advance to welcome and forgive.

Of these things Mistrial made his wife aware, and it was then that the rainbow departed. His arguments were as revolting as the cynicism they exhaled. But she made no attempt to combat them. Since she had seen her father she had felt a sorrow for him that Mistrial's altered demeanor had given her time to heed. She knew that his attitude was due to her defiance of his express commands, but she had no reason to suppose that he had any other objection to her husband than such as his poverty might have caused or instinctive antipathy might bring. But now, her own experience aiding, she knew that he had been right; and, as he seemed feeble and dispassionate, in answer to Mistrial's arguments she tied her bonnet-strings and went. It was early in the afternoon when she started, it was night when she returned.

Mistrial had been waiting for her, and when she entered the room in which he sat he rose eagerly and aided her with her wrap. He was impatient, she could see; and she was impatient also.

"Why did you not tell me of Guy's sister?" she began, at once.

And as he answered nothing she continued: "Years ago I knew of what she died; it was only to-day I learned that it was you who murdered her."

"It is a lie."

"Oh, protest. I knew you would."

"From whom is it you heard this thing? Not from your father, I am sure." As Mistrial spoke he gazed at her inquisitorially with shrewd, perplexing eyes.

"What does it matter?" she answered. Her head was thrown back, her lips compressed. "What does it matter since the charge is true?"

"But it is false," he cried; "it is a wanton lie. Your father never could have stated it."

"Ah, but he did, though; and Guy was there to substantiate what he said."

"Guy!" As he pronounced her cousin's name there came into his face an expression which she knew and which she had learned to dread. "Madam, you mean your lover, I suppose. And it is his ipse dixit you accept in preference to mine?"

"Mistrial, you know he is not my lover."

"I know he was in love with you, and you with him."

"So he was; so he is, I think; and it was not until this night I saw my own mistake."

"Voilà!" said Roland, suddenly calmed. He paused a second, and after eying the polish of his finger-nails, affected to flick a speck of dust from his sleeve. "Your cousin is mad," he added.

"He is sane as—" and Justine hesitated for a simile.

"His mother, you mean. Were you never aware that insanity is hereditary? If his sister—presupposing that the accusation which he formulates against me was originally advanced by her—if his sister—whom, by the way, I never saw but once—if his sister accused me of complicity, then she suffered from the hereditary taint as well. If I was guilty of what your cousin charges, why was I not arrested, tried, and sentenced? But are you such a dolt you cannot see that Guy is mad—mad not only by nature, but crazed by jealousy as well. You say you know he loves you. You have even the candor to admit that you love him! Now ask yourself what would any impartial hearer deduce from statements such as yours?"

"My father was an impartial hearer, and he—"

"But how is it possible to be so blind? Can you not see that your cousin has prejudiced him against me? I said, impartial hearer. But let the matter drop. I tell you the charge is false; believe it or not, as you prefer. There is, however, just this in the matter: if the charge is made again, I will have your cousin under arrest. You forget that there is such a thing as libel still."

Again he paused, and strove to collect himself; there was a design in the carpet which appeared to interest him very much, but presently he looked up again.

"Now tell me," he said, "what did your father say?"

"Nothing, save what he said before."

"Nothing?"

"Nothing that you would care to hear." Her eyes roamed from the neighbourly ceiling over to him and back again. "He said," she added, "that if I persisted in living with you his money would go to my child, if I had one; if I had none, then to Guy."

"Were you alone with him when he said this, or was Guy, as you call him, there?"

"No, I was alone with him; Guy came later."

"And is he aware of this provision?"

For all response Justine shrugged her shoulders.

"Does he know it, I ask you?"

"He does not," she answered. "Father told me that he never would, until the will was read."

"H'm." And for a moment Mistrial mused. Then presently he smiled—yet was it a smile?—a look that an hallucinated monk in a medieval abbey might have seen on that imaginary demon who, flitting by him, the forefinger outstretched, whispered as he vanished through the wall, "Thou art damned, dear friend! thou art damned!" "H'm," he repeated; "and in view of the provisions of your father's will, will you tell me why is it that you are without a child?"

As he spoke he had arisen, and, smiling still, though now as were he questioning her in regard to the state of the weather, he looked into her eyes. She had drawn yet further back into the chair in which she sat; a deadly sickness overcame her; to her head there mounted the nausea of each one of his many misdeeds. The memory of the blow of the week before, one which, despite her seeming forbearance, had not ceased to rankle, returned to her; and with it, one after another in swift succession, she rememorated the offences of the past. But soon she too was on her feet and fronted him. "Why is it I am without a child?" she repeated. Her voice was low and clear, and between each word she permitted a little pause to intervene. "Why is it?"

The subtlety of his reproach battening on nerves already overwrought was exciting her as nothing had done before. "It is you," she cried, "who are to blame. What have you done with your youth? What have you done with your manhood? Look at me, Roland Mistrial! If I have borne you no child it is because monsters never engender." As she spoke, with one gesture she tore her bodice down. Her breast, palpitant with health and anger too, heaving at the sheer injustice of his reproach, confronted and confuted him. "It is there that women have their strength; tell me, if you can, what have you done with yours?"

And thereat, with a look a princess might give to a lackey who had dared to question her, she turned and left him where he stood.

The next day he tried to make his peace with her. In this he succeeded, or flattered himself he had, for subsequently she consented to accompany him to the play. And as she sat in the stalls it was of these things that she thought.

II.

The information which Mistrial gleaned concerning the provisions of his father-in-law's will was bitter in his mouth. On the morrow he gave some time to thought—he read too a little. The taunt which Justine had flung at him, bit; and with the idea of dulling the hurt and of ministering also to his own refreshment, he consulted a book which treated of certain conditions of the nervous system, and a work on medical jurisprudence as well. But literature of that kind is notoriously unsatisfactory. It may suggest, yet the questions which it prompts remain unanswered. Roland put the volumes down: they were productions of genius, no doubt, but to him they were nothing more. From the pursuit of exact knowledge he turned and looked out into the street.

The hour then was midway in one of those green afternoons which we are apt to fancy the adjunct of lands we never see, and as he looked he saw astride a bay hunter a man ambling cautiously over the stones. From the roofs opposite a breath of lilacs came, and a breeze that was neither cool nor warm loitered on its way from the river beyond. Mistrial let the breeze, the fragrance, the fulfilment of spring, pass unnoticed. The bay hunter had caught his eye: it seemed to him that an argument with an imperative horse was just the thing he needed most, and a little later he secured a cob from a stable on the street above.

The cob was docile enough, affecting once only to regard a sewer-grating in the bridle-path as a strange, unhallowed thing which it was needful to avoid. But the initial shy was the last. The spur gave him such a nip that during the remainder of the ride, whatever distasteful object he may have encountered, he gave no outward evidence of abhorrence. He had an easy canter, a long and swinging trot; and now on one, now on the other, they passed through and out of the Park, and on beyond the brand-new edifices that line Seventh Avenue, to that scantier outlying district where the Harlem begins and the city ends. And here as he was about to turn he noticed a gig such as physicians affect. In it was a negro driving, and at his side sat Justine's cousin, Guy.

"H'm!" mused Mistrial; "judging by the locality, his patients must be the last people in the city." At the moment the feebleness of the jest pleasured him; then simultaneously the unforgotten hatred crackled in his breast. At each one of the important epochs of his life that man had stood in his way. It was he that had forced him from college at the moment when honors were within his reach. It was he that had kept him from his father's side at the time when he might have saved his father's estate. It was he that had come between Dunellen and himself at the hour when he could have persuaded Justine's father to give him Justine's hand. It was he that had forced him to elope with her. It was because of him that he was now enjoying the small miseries of the shabby genteel. It was he, unless Providence now intervened, who would inherit the wealth he had toiled to make his own. And it was he who the day before had again crossed and halted in his path.

These premises, however colored, were logical enough in this—the natural deduction sprang out and greeted the eye. And, as they flashed before him, Mistrial saw himself rinsing out each one in blood squeezed from Thorold's throat. In the fury which suddenly beset him he could have found the strength, the courage it may be, to have torn him from the gig in which he sat, to have trampled on him with horse's hoofs, bent over and beat him as he writhed on the ground, and exulted and jubilated in the doing of it. Then indeed, though he swung for it, the ultimate victory would be his. If he stamped Thorold out of existence, though his own went with it, he would not have suffered wholly in vain; in facing the gallows he would have the joy of knowing that even were he prevented from bathing in the Dunellen millions, so was Thorold too.

But when he looked out from himself his enemy had disappeared. A woman in an open landau passed and bowed. Mechanically Mistrial raised his hat. To every intent and purpose he was self-possessed—occupied, if at all, but with those threads of fancy that float in and out the mind. As he raised his hat, he smiled; the woman might have thought herself the one it gave him the greatest pleasure to salute. Her carriage had not advanced the jump of a cat before he had forgotten that she lived. But no one can turn his brain into a stage, create for it, and feel a drama such as he had without some outward manifestation, be it merely a strangled oath. On the horse he rode his knees had tightened, he gave a dig with the spur, and went careering down the street. In that part of New York you are at liberty to cover a mile in two minutes. Roland covered thirty squares at breakneck speed.

Presently he drew the animal in and suffered him to walk. During the run he had had no time to think; he had been occupied only in keeping the horse he rode out of the way of vehicles, and in preventing that possible cropper which comes when we expect it least. But as the cob began to walk, the present returned to him with a rush. About the animal's neck the fretting of the reins had produced a lather; the breeze had died away. Mistrial felt overheated too, and he drew out a handkerchief and wiped his face. Even while he drew it from his pocket an idea came to him, fluttered for a second as ideas will, and before he got the handkerchief back it had gone, leaving him just a trifled dazed. But in a moment he called to it, and at his bidding it returned. It was minute, barely fledged as yet; but as the horse jogged on, little by little it expanded, and to such an extent that before he reached the park its pinions stretched from earth to sky. Whoso is visited with inspirations knows with what diabolical swiftness they can enlarge and grow. When Mistrial put the horse back in the stable the idea which at first he had but dimly intercepted possessed him utterly. It succeeded even in detaining his step: he walked up the street instead of down; at a crossing he hesitated; night had come, and as he loitered there, suddenly the whole avenue was bright as day. The vengeance which not an hour before he could have wreaked on Thorold seemed now remote and paltry too. There need be no shedding of blood, no scandal, no newspaper notoriety, no police, no coroner to sit upon a corpse, no jury to bring a verdict in. There need be nothing of this: a revenge of that order was in bad taste, ill-judged as well. To make a man really suffer, sudden death was as a balm in comparison to some subtle torment that should gnaw at the springs of life, retreat a moment, and then returning make them ache again, and still again, forever his whole life through. The French woman is not so ill-advised when she pitches a cup of vitriol in her betrayer's face. In Spain, in Italy even, they stab; the deed is done; the culprit has had no chance to experience anger, pain even, or remorse. He is dead. The curtain falls. But a revenge that blasts and corrodes, one that leaves the victim living, sound in body and in limb, and yet consumed by an inextinguishable regret, burning with tortures from which he can never escape—a thing like that is the work, not of an apprentice, but of a master in crime. Yet when the victim receives that cup of vitriol, not from another's hands, but from his own; when he has been lured into devastating his own self;—it is no longer a question of either apprentice or of master: it is the artist that has been at work. To gain the Dunellen millions was to Mistrial a matter of paramount importance; but to gain them through the instrumentality of the man whom he hated as no one ever hates to-day, particularly when that man was the one to whom those millions were provisionally bequeathed, when he was one whom Mistrial—justly or unjustly, it matters not—fancied and believed was plotting for them; to gain them, not only through him, but through his unwitting, unintentional agency, through an act which, so soon as he learned its purport, all his life through he would regret and curse;—no, that were indeed a revenge and a reparation too. And as he thought of it there entered his eyes a look perplexing and enervating—that look which demons share with sphinxes and the damned.

III.

During the two years which Mistrial had passed in the society of his wife, opportunities of studying her there had been in plenty. He knew her to be docile and headstrong; weak, if at all, but with that weakness that comes of lassitude; violent when provoked, prone to forgive, sensitive, impulsive, yet obdurate; in brief, the type of woman that may be entreated, but never coerced. He knew her faults so well he could have enumerated them one after the other on his finger-tips: her qualities, however, had impressed him less; it may be that he had accepted them as a matter of course. He was aware that she was honest; he had noticed that she was capable of much self-sacrifice; of other characteristics he had given little heed. It goes without the telling, that in regard to what is known as jealousy he had not suffered even an evanescent disquietude. And that night and during the morning that followed, as he occupied himself in nursing the idea which had visited him on horseback, that particular fact occurred to him more than once. But one does not need to be a conspirator to understand that the steadiest virtue is as susceptible of vice as iron is of rust.

Justine had announced that her cousin was still in love with her; she had announced with equal distinctness that she recognized her own mistake; while for himself he was convinced that she no longer cared. To these things he added certain deductions which his experience of men and women permitted him to draw; and had the result they presented been made to order, it could not have fitted more perfectly into the scheme which he had devised.

It was then high noon. Through the window came the irresistible breath of a rose in bloom. As he left the house it surrounded him in the street. He smiled a greeting at it. "I have spring in my favor," he mused, and presently boarded a car.

The principles of successful enterprise may be summarized as consisting of a minute regard for details, and an apparent absence of zeal. Mistrial's many mistakes had taught him the one and trained him in the other. When the car he had taken reached the Gilsey House, he alighted, hailed a four-wheeler, stationed it in such a manner that it commanded a view of the adjacent street, coached the driver in regard to a signal he might give, entered the cab, lit a cigarette, and prepared to wait.

In that neighborhood there are four or five basement houses of the style that is affectioned by milliners, dentists, and physicians. One of these particularly claimed Mistrial's attention. He saw a woman in gray enter it, and almost simultaneously a woman come out; then a man leading a child went in; and in a little while the first woman reappeared. Mistrial glanced at his watch; it lacked a minute of one. "He has a larger practice than I thought," he reflected. The woman in gray had now nearly reached the cab in which he sat, and from sheer force of habit he was preparing to scrutinize her as she passed, when the door of the house reopened and Thorold appeared on the step. He looked up the street, then down. He had his hat on, and his every-day air. In a second Mistrial had drawn the curtain and was peering through the opening at the side. He saw Thorold leave the step and turn toward Fifth Avenue; he signalled to the driver, and the cab moved on.

At the corner Thorold turned again, the cab at his heels, and Mistrial saw that the physician was moving in the direction of Madison Square. It occurred to him that Thorold might be going to Mr. Dunellen's, and on the block below, as the latter crossed the asphalt, he made sure of it. But opposite the Brunswick the cab stopped; Thorold was entering the restaurant.

Cold chicken looks attractive in print. A minute or two later, as Mistrial examined the bill of fare, he ordered some for himself; he ordered also a Demidorf salad,—a compound of artichokes' hearts and truffles, familiarly known as Half-Mourning,—and until the waiter returned hid himself behind a paper. Thorold meanwhile, who was seated at an adjoining table, must have ordered something which required longer preparation, for Mistrial finished the salad before the physician was served. But Mistrial was in no hurry; he had a pint of claret brought him, and sipped it leisurely. Now and then he glanced over at Thorold, and twice he caught his eye. At last Thorold called for his bill. Mistrial paid his own, and presently followed him out into the street. When both reached the sidewalk, Mistrial, who was a trifle in the rear, touched him on the arm.

"Thorold," he said; and the physician turned, but there was nothing engaging in his attitude: he held his head to one side, about his lips was a compression, a contraction in his eyes; one arm was pendent, the other pressed to his waistcoat, and the shoulder of that arm was slightly raised. He looked querulous and annoyed—a trifle startled, too.

"Thorold," Mistrial repeated, "give me a moment, will you?"

The physician raised the arm that he had pressed against his waistcoat, and, with four fingers straightened and the fifth askew, stroked an imaginary whisker.

"It is about Justine," Mistrial continued. "She is out of sorts; I want you to see her."

"Ah!" And Thorold looked down and away.

"Yes, I had intended to speak to Dr. McMasters; but when by the merest chance I saw you in there I told myself that, whatever our differences might be, there was no one who would understand the case more readily than you."

As Mistrial spoke he imitated the discretion of his enemy; he looked down and away. The next moment, however, both were gazing into each other's face.

"H'm." Thorold, as he stared, seemed to muse. "I saw her the other day," he said, at last; "she looked well enough then."

"But can't a person look well and yet be out of sorts?"

Mistrial was becoming angry, and he showed it. It was evident, however, that his irritation was caused less by the man to whom he spoke than by the physician whom he was seeking to consult. This Thorold seemed to grasp, for he answered perplexedly:

"After what has happened I don't see very well how I can go to your house."

"Look here, Thorold: the past is over and done with—ill done, you will say, and I admit it. Be that as it may, it has gone. At the same time there is no reason why any shadow of it should fall on Justine. She is really in need of some one's advice. Can you not give it to her?"

"Certainly," Thorold answered, "I can do that;" and he looked very sturdy as he said it. "Only—"

"Only what? If you can't go as a friend, at least you might go as a physician."

Thorold's hand had slid from his cheek to his chin, and he nibbled reflectively at a finger-nail.

"Very good," he said; "I will go to her. Is she to be at home this afternoon?"

"The evening would be better, I think. Unless, of course—" and Mistrial made a gesture as though to imply that, if Thorold's evening were engaged, a visit in the afternoon might be attempted.

But the suggestion presumably was acceptable. Thorold drew out a note-book, at which he glanced.

"And I say," Mistrial continued, "I wish—you see, it is a delicate matter; Justine is very sensitive—I wish you wouldn't say you met me. Just act as though—"

"Give yourself no uneasiness, sir." Thorold had replaced the note-book and looked up again in Mistrial's face. "I never mention your name." And thereat, with a toss of the head, he dodged an omnibus and crossed the street.

For a moment Mistrial gazed after him, then he turned, and presently he was ordering a glass of brandy at the Brunswick bar.

It was late that night when he reached his home. During the days that followed he had no fixed hours at all. Several times he entered the apartment with the smallest amount of noise that was possible, and listened at the sitting-room door. At last he must have heard something that pleased him, for as he sought his own room he smiled. "Maintenant, mon cher, je te tiens."

The next day he surprised Justine by informing her that he intended to pay a visit to a relative. He was gone a week.

IV.

That night the stars, dim and distant, were scattered like specks of frost on some wide, blue window-pane. At intervals a shiver of wheels crunching the resistant snow stirred the lethargy of the street, and at times a rumble accentuated by the chill of winter mounted gradually, and passed on in diminishing vibrations. Within, a single light, burning scantily, diffused through the room the drowsiness of a spell. In the bed was Justine, her eyes dilated, her face attenuated and pinched. One hand that lay on the coverlid was clinched so tightly that the nails must have entered the flesh. Presently she moaned, and a trim little woman issued from a corner with the noiseless wariness of a rat. As she passed before the night-light, the silhouette of a giantess, fabulously obese, jumped out and vanished from the wall. For a moment she scrutinized her charge, burrowing into her, as it were, with shrewd yet kindly eyes. Again a moan escaped the sufferer, the wail of one whose agony is lancinating—one that ascended in crescendos and terminated in a cry of such utter helplessness, and therewith of such insistent pain, that the nurse caught the hand that lay on the coverlid, and unlocking the fingers stroked and held it in her own. "There, dear heart—there, I know."

Ah, yes, she knew very well. She had not passed ten years of her existence tending women in travail for the fun of it. And as she took Justine's hand and stroked it, she knew that in a little while the agony, acuter still, would lower her charge into that vestibule of death where Life appears. Whether or not Justine was to cross that silent threshold, whether happily she would find it barred, whether it would greet and keep her and hold her there, whether indeed it would let the child go free, an hour would tell, or two at most.

But there were preparations to be made. The nurse left the bed and moved out into the hall. In a room near by, Mistrial, occupied with some advertisements in the Post, sat companioned by a physician who was reading a book which he had written himself. At the footfall of the nurse the latter left the room. Presently he returned. "Everything is going nicely," he announced, and placidly resumed his seat.

It was the fourth time in two hours that he had made that same remark. Mistrial said nothing. He was gazing through the paper he held at the wall opposite, and out of it into the future beyond.

Since that day, the previous spring, on which he had set out to visit a relative, many things had happened, yet but few that were of importance to him. On his return from the trip, during one fleeting second, for the first time since he had known Justine, it seemed to him that she avoided his eyes. To this, in other circumstances, he would have given no thought whatever; as matters were, it made him feel that his excursion should not be regarded as time ill-spent. Whether it had been wholly serviceable to his project, he could not at the time decide. He waited, however, very patiently, but he seldom waited within the apartment walls. At that period he developed a curious facility for renewing relations with former friends. Once he took a run to Chicago with an Englishman he had known in Japan; and once, with the brother of a lady who had married into the Baxter branch of the house of Mistrial, he went on a fishing trip to Canada. These people he did not bring to call on his wife. He seemed to act as though solitude were grateful to her. Save Mrs. Metuchen,

Thorold at that time was her only visitor, and the visits of that gentleman Mistrial encouraged in every way that he could devise. Through meetings that, parenthetically, were more frequent on the stair or in the hallway than anywhere else, the two men, through sheer force of circumstances, dropped into an exchange of salutations—remarks about the weather, reciprocal inquiries on the subject of each other's health, which, wholly formal on Thorold's part, were from Mistrial always civil and aptly put. After all, was he not the host? and was it not for him to show particular courtesy to anyone whom his wife received?

To her, meanwhile, his attitude was little short of perfection itself. He was considerate, foresighted, and unobtrusive—a course of conduct which frightened her a little. Two or three months after he had struck her in the face she made—à propos of nothing at all—an announcement which brought a trace of color to her cheeks.

The following afternoon he happened to be entering the house as Dr. Thorold was leaving it. Instead of greeting him in the nice and amiable fashion which he had adopted, and which Thorold had ended by accepting as a matter of course, he halted and looked at the physician through half-closed eyes. Thorold nodded, cavalierly enough it is true, and was about to pass on; but this Mistrial prevented. He planted himself squarely in his way, and stuck his hands in his pockets.

"Mrs. Mistrial has no further need of you," he said. "Send your bill to me."

He spoke from the tips of his lips, with the air and manner of one dismissing a lackey. At the moment nothing pertinent could have occurred to Thorold. He stared at Mistrial, dumbly perplexed, and plucked at his cuff. Mistrial nodded as who should say, "Put that in your pipe;" and before Thorold recovered his self-possession he had passed up the stairs and on and out of sight.

It was then that season in which July has come and is going. The city was hot; torrid at noonday, sultry and enervating at night. Fifth Avenue and the adjacent precincts were empty. Each one of the brown-stone houses had a Leah-like air of desertion. The neighborhood of Madison and of Union Squares was peopled by men with large eyes and small feet, by women so deftly painted that, like Correggio, they could have exclaimed, "Anch' io son pittore." In brief, the Southern invasion had begun, and New York had ceased to be habitable.

But Newport has charms of its own; and to that lovely city by the water Mistrial induced his wife; and there, until summer had departed, and autumn too, they rested and waited. During those months he was careful of her: so pleasantly so, so studious of what she did and of what she ate, that for the first time since the honeymoon she might have, had she tried, felt at ease with him again. But there were things that prevented this—faith destroyed and the regret of it. Oh, indeed she had regrets in plenty; some even for her father; and, unknown to Mistrial, once or twice she wrote him such letters as a daughter may write. She had never been in sympathy with him; as a child he had coerced her needlessly; when she was older he had preached; later, divining that lack of sympathy, he had striven through kindlier ways to counteract it. But he had failed; and Justine, aiding in the endeavor, had failed as well. When father and child do not stand hand-in-hand a fibre is wanting that should be there.

In December Mistrial and his wife returned to town. A date was approaching, and there was the layette to be prepared. Hour after hour Justine's fingers sped. The apartment became a magazine of swaddling-clothes. One costume in particular, a worsted sack that was not much larger than a coachman's glove, duplicated and repeated itself in varying and tender hues. Occasionally Mistrial would pick one up and examine it furtively. To his vagabond fancy it suggested a bag in which gold would be.

But now the hour was reached. And as Mistrial sat staring into the future, the goal to which he had striven kept looming nearer and ever nearer yet. Only the day before he had learned that Dunellen was failing. And what a luxury it would be to him when the old man died and the will was read! Such a luxury did it appear, that unconsciously he manifested his contentment by that sound the glutton makes at the mention of delicious food.

His companion—the physician—turned and nodded. "I know what you are thinking about," he announced; and with the rapt expression of a seer, half to Mistrial, half to the ceiling, "It is always the case," he continued; "I never knew a father yet that did not wonder what the child would be; and the mothers, oh! the mothers! Some of them know all about it beforehand: they want a girl, and a girl it will be; or they want a boy, and a boy they are to have. I remember one dear, good soul who was so positive she was to have a boy that she had all the linen marked with the name she had chosen for him. H'm. It turned out to be twins—both girls. And I remember—"

But Mistrial had ceased to listen. He was off again discounting the inheritance in advance—discounting, too, the diabolism of his revenge. The latter, indeed, was unique, and withal so grateful, that now the consummation was at hand it fluttered his pulse like wine. He had ravened when first he learned the tenour of the will, and his soul had been bitter; but no sooner had this thing occurred to him than it resolved itself into a delight. To his disordered fancy its provisions held both vitriol and opopanax—the one for Thorold, the other for himself.

The doctor meanwhile was running on as doctors do. "Yes," Mistrial heard him say, "she was most unhappy; no woman likes a rival, and when that rival is her own maid, matters are not improved. For my part, the moment I saw how delicate she was, I thought, though I didn't dare to say so, I thought her husband had acted with great forethought. The maid was strong as an ox, and in putting her in the same condition as his wife he had simply and solely supplied her with a wet-nurse. But then, at this time particularly, women are so unreasonable. Not your good lady—a sweeter disposition—"

Whatever encomium he intended to make remained unfinished. From the room beyond a cry filtered; he turned hastily and disappeared. The cry subsided; but presently, as though in the interval the sufferer had found new strength or new torture, it rose more stridently than before. And as the rumor of it augmented and increased, a phrase of the physician's returned to Mistrial. "Everything is going very nicely," he told himself, and began to pace the floor.

A fraction of an hour passed, a second, and a third. The cry now had changed singularly; it had lost its penetrating volume, it had sunk into the rasping moan of one dreaming in a fever. Suddenly that ceased, the silence was complete, and Mistrial, a trifle puzzled, moved out into the hall. There he caught again the murmur of her voice. This time she was talking very rapidly, in a continuous flow of words. From where he stood Mistrial could not hear what she was saying, and he groped on tip-toe down the hall. As he reached the door of the room in which she was, the sweet and heavy odor of chloroform came out and met him there; but still the flow of words continued uninterruptedly, one after the other, with the incoherence of a nightmare monologuing in a corpse. Then, without transition, in the very middle of a word, a cry of the supremest agony rang out, drowning another, which was but a vague complaint.

"It's a boy," the nurse exclaimed.

And Justine through a rift of consciousness caught and detained the speech. "So much the better," she moaned; "he will never give birth."

V.

"We brought nothing into this world, and it is certain we can carry nothing out. The Lord gave, and the Lord hath taken away: blessed be the name of the Lord."

To this, Mistrial, garbed in black, responded discreetly, "Amen."

He was standing opposite the bier. At his side was Justine. Before him Dr. Gonfallon, rector of the Church of Gethsemane,—of which the deceased had been warden,—was conducting the funeral rites. To the left was Thorold. Throughout the length and breadth of the drawing-room other people stood—a sprinkling of remote connections, former constituents, members of the bar and of the church, a few politicians; these, together with a handful of the helpless to whom the dead statesman had been trustee, counsellor too, and guide, had assembled there in honor of his memory. At the door, sharpening a pencil, was a representative of the Associated Press.

For the past few days obituaries of the Hon. Paul Dunellen varied from six inches to a column in length. One journal alone had been circumspect. No mention of the deceased had appeared in its issues. But in politics that journal had differed with him—a fact which accounted sufficiently for its silence. In the others, however, through biographies more or less exact, fitting tributes had been paid. TheWorld gave his picture.

Yet now, as Dr. Gonfallon, in words well calculated to impress, dwelt on the virtues of him that had gone, the tributes of the newspapers seemed perfunctory and trite. Decorously, as was his custom, he began with a platitude. Death, that is terrible to the sinner, radiant to the Christian, imposing to all, was here, he declared, but the dusk of a beautiful day which in departing disclosed cohorts of the Eternal beckoning from their glorious realm. Yet soon he warmed to his work, and eulogies of the deceased fell from him in sonorous periods, round and empty. He spoke of the nobility of his character, the loyalty he displayed, not to friends alone, but to foes as well. He spoke of that integrity in every walk of life which had won for him the title of Honest Paul—a title an emperor might crave and get not. He spoke too of the wealth he had acquired, and drew a moral from the unostentatiousness of his charities, the simplicity of his ways. He dwelt at length on the fact that, however multiple the duties of his station had been, his duty to his Maker was ever first. Then, after a momentary digression, in which he stated how great was the loss of such as he, he alluded to the daughter he had left, to that daughter's husband, sorely afflicted himself, yet, with a manliness worthy of his historic name, comforting the orphan who needed all his comfort now; and immediately from these things he lured another moral—an appeal to fortitude and courage; and winding up with the customary exordium, asked of Death where was its sting.

Where was it indeed? A day or two later Mistrial found time to think of that question and of other matters as well. It was then six weeks since the birth of the child, and Justine, fairer than ever before, was ministering to it in the adjacent room. Now and again he caught the shrill vociferation of its vague complaints. It was a feeble infant, lacking in vitality, distressingly hideous; but it lived, and though it died the next minute, its life had sufficed.

Already the will had been read—a terse document, and to the point; precisely such an one as you would have expected a jurist to make. By it the testator devised his property, real and personal, of whatever nature, kind, and description he died seized, to his former partners in trust for the eldest child of his daughter Justine, to its heirs, executors, and assigns forever. In the event of his daughter's demise without issue, then over, to Guy Thorold, M.D.

No, the sting concerning which Dr. Gonfallon had inquired was to Mistrial undiscerned. There was indeed a prick of it in the knowledge that if the old man had lasted much longer it might have been tough work to settle the bills; but that was gone now: Honest Paul paid all his debts, and he had not shirked at Nature's due. He was safely and securely dead, six feet under ground at that, and his millions were absolute in his grandson. Yes, absolute. At the thought of it Mistrial laughed. The goal to which for years he had striven was touched and exceeded. He had thrown the vitriol, the opopanax was his.

We all of us pretend to forgive, to overlook, to condone, we pretend even to sympathize with, our enemy. Nay, in refraining from an act that could injure him who has injured us, we are quite apt to consider ourselves the superior of our foe, and not a little inclined to rise to the heights of self-laudatory quotation too. It is an antique virtue, that of forbearance; it is Biblical, nobly Arthurian, and chivalresque. But when we smile at an injury, it is for policy's sake—because we fear, rarely because we truly forgive, more rarely yet because of indifference. Our magnanimity is cowardice. It takes a brave man to wreak a brave revenge.

Mistrial made few pretensions to the virtues which you and I possess. He was relentless as a Sioux, and he was treacherous as the savage is; he had no taste for fair and open fight. However his blood had boiled at the tableau of imaginary wrongs, however fitting the opportunity might have been on the afternoon when he met his enemy at the city's fringe, he had the desire but not the courage to annihilate him there. But later, when the possibility which he had intercepted came, he fêted, he coaxed it; and now that the hour of triumph had rung, his heart was glad. In the disordered closets of his brain he saw Thorold ravening at the trap into which he had fallen, and into which, in falling, he had lost the wherewithal to call the world his own. Ten million in exchange for an embrace! Verily, mused Mistrial, he will account it exceeding dear. And at the thought of what Thorold's frenzy must be, at the picture which he drew of him cursing his own imprudence and telling himself again and again, until the repetition turned into mania, that that imprudence could never be undone, he exulted and laughed aloud.

Money, said Vespasian, has no odor. To our acuter nostrils it has: so nauseating even can it be, that we would rather be flung in the Potter's-field than catch the faintest whiff. But Mistrial, for all the sensitiveness that ancestry is supposed to bring, must have agreed with the Roman. To him it was the woof of every hope; whatever its provenance, it was an Open Sesame to the paradise of the ideal. He would have drawn it with his teeth from a dung-heap, only he would have done it at night.

There are men that can steal a fortune, yet can never cheat at cards, and Mistrial was one of their race; he could not openly dishonor himself in petty ways. Many a scoundrel has a pride of his own. It is both easy and difficult to compare a bandit to a sneak-thief, Napoleon to Cartouche. Mistrial had nothing of the Napoleon about him, and he was lacking even in the strength which Cartouche possessed. But among carpet highwaymen commend me to his peer.

And now, as he thought of the will, Gonfallon's query recurred to him, and he asked himself where was that sting? Not in the present, surely—for that from a bitterness had changed to a delight; and as for the future, each instant of it was sentient with invocations, fulfilled to the tips with the surprises of dream. The day he had claimed but a share in; the morrow was wholly his. He could have a dwelling in Mayfair and a marble palace on the Mediterranean Sea. For a scrap of paper he would never miss there was a haunt of ghosts dozing on the Grand Canal. In spring, when Paris is at her headiest, there, near that Triumphal Arch which overlooks the Elysian Fields, stood,entre cour et jardin, an hotel which he already viewed as his own. And when he wearied of the Old World, there was the larger and fuller life of the New. There was Peru, there was Mexico and Ecuador; and in those Italys of the Occident were girls whose lips said, Drink me; whose eyes were of chrysoberyl and of jade. Ah, oui, les femmes; tant que le monde tournera il n'y aura que ça. With blithe anticipation he hummed the air and snapped his fingers as Capoul was wont to do. At last he saw himself the Roland Mistrial that should have been, prodigal of gold, sultanesque of manner, fêted, courted, welcomed, past-master in the lore and art of love.

There were worlds still to be conquered; and before his hair grizzled and the furrows came he felt conscious of the possession of a charm that should make those worlds his own. He had waited indeed; he had toiled and manœuvred; but now the great clock we call Opportunity had struck. Let him but ask, and it would be given. Wishes were spaniels; he had but a finger to raise, and they fawned at his feet. And then, as those vistas of which we have all caught a glimpse rose in melting splendor and swooned again through sheer excesses of their own delights, suddenly he bethought him of the multiples of one and of two.

Heretofore he had taken it for granted that if Dunellen left the estate to his grandchild the income accruing therefrom would, until the grandchild came of age, pass through his own paternal hands. And in taking this for granted he had recalled the fable that deals not of the prodigal son, but rather of the prodigal father. That income should spin. By a simple mathematical process than with which no one was more familiar, he calculated that, at five per cent, ten million would represent a rent-roll of five hundred thousand per annum. Of that amount a fraction would suffice to Justine and to her son. The rest—well, the rest he knew of what uses he could put it to.

But now, suddenly, with that abruptness with which disaster looms, there came to him a doubt. He rememorated the provisions of the will, and in them he discerned unprompted some tenet of law or of custom which, during the legal infancy of the child, might inhibit the trustees from paying over any larger amount than was needful for its maintenance and support. Then at once the fabric of his dreams dissolved. The vitriol had corroded, but the savor of the opopanax had gone. For a little while he tormented his mustache and nibbled feverishly at a finger-nail. To see one's self the dupe of one's own devices is never a pleasant sight. Again he interrogated what smattering of law he possessed; but the closer he looked, the clearer it seemed to be that in its entirety the income of the estate could not pass through his hands. From five hundred thousand the trustees might in their judgment diminish it to some such pocket-money as ten; they could even reduce it to five; and, barring an action, he might be unable to persuade them that the sum was absurd. The idea, nude and revolting as Truth ever is, raised him to an unaccustomed height of rage; he would not be balked, he declared to himself; he would have that money or—

Or what? The contingency which he then interviewed, one which issued unsummoned from some cavern in his mind, little by little assumed a definite shape. He needed no knowledge of the law to tell him that he was that brat's heir. Did it die at that very moment the estate became absolute in him. There would be no trustees then to dole the income out. The ten millions would be his own. As for the trustees, they could deduct their commission and retire with it to New Jersey—to hell if it pleased them more. But the estate would be his. That there was no gainsaying. Meanwhile, there was the brat. He was a feeble child; yet such, Mistrial understood, had Methusaleh been. He might live forever, or die on the morrow. And why not that night?

As this query came to him, he eyed its advance. It was yet some distance away, but as it approached he considered it from every side. And of sides, parenthetically, it had many. And still it advanced: when it started, its movements were so slow they had been hardly perceptible; nevertheless it had made some progress; then surer on its feet it tried to run; it succeeded in the effort; at each step it grew sturdier, swifter in speed; and now that it reached him it was with such a rush that he was overpowered by its force.

He rose from his seat. For a moment he hesitated. To his forehead and about his ears a moisture had come. He drew out a handkerchief; it was of silk, he noticed—one that he brought from France. Absently he drew it across his face; its texture had detained his thought. Then on tip-toe he moved out into the corridor and peered into the room at the end of the hall.

It was dimly lighted, but soon he accustomed himself to the shadows and fumbled them with his eyes. On the bed Justine lay; sleep had overtaken her; her head was aslant on the pillow, her lips half closed; the fingers of one hand cushioned her neck; the other hand, outstretched, rested on the edge of a cradle. She had been rocking it, perhaps. From the floor above sank the sauntering tremolo of a flute, very sweet in the distance, muffled by the ceiling and wholly subdued. In the street a dray was passing, belated and clamorous on the cobblestones. But now, as Mistrial ventured in, these things must have lulled Justine into yet deeper sleep; her breath came and went with the semibreves a leaf uses when it whispers to the night; and as he moved nearer and bent over her the whiteness of her breast rose and fell in unison with that breath. Yes, surely she slept, but it was with that wary sleep that dogs and mothers share. A movement of that child's and she might awake, alert at once, her senses wholly recovered, her mind undazed.

Mistrial, assured of her slumber, turned from the bed to the cradle, and for a minute, two perhaps, he stood, the eyebrows raised, the handkerchief pendent in his hand, contemplating the occupant. And it was this bundle of flesh and blood, this lobster-hued animal, that lacked the intelligence a sightless kitten has,—it was this that should debar him! Allons donc!

His face had grown livid, and his hand shook just a little; not with fear, however, though if it were it must have been the temerity of his own courage that frightened him. At the handkerchief which he held he glanced again; one twist of it round that infant's throat, a minute in which to hold it taut, and it would be back in his pocket, leaving strangulation and death behind, yet not a mark to tell the tale. One minute only he needed, two at most; he bent nearer, and as he bent he looked over at his wife; but still she slept, her breath coming and going with the same regular cadence as before, the whiteness of her breast still heaving; then very gently, with fingers that were nervously assured, he ran the handkerchief under the infant's neck: but however deftly he had done it, the chill of the silk must have troubled the child; its under lip quivered, then both compressed, the flesh about the cheek-bones furrowed, the mouth relaxed, and from it issued the whimper of unconscious plaint. The call may have stirred the mother in some dream, for a smile hovered in her features; yet immediately her eyes opened, she half rose, her hand fell to her side, and, reaching out, she caught and held the infant to her.

"My darling," she murmured; and as the child, soothed already, drowsed back again into slumber, she turned to where her husband stood. "What is it?"

From above, the tremolo of the flute still descended; but the dray long since had passed, and the street now was quiet.

"What is it?" she repeated. She seemed more surprised than pleased to see him there.

Mistrial, balked in the attempt, had straightened himself; he looked annoyed and restless.

"Nothing," he answered, and thrust the handkerchief back in his pocket, as a bandit sheathes his dirk. "Nothing. I heard that bastard bawling, and I came in to make him stop."

"Bastard? Is it in that way you speak of your child?"

As she said this she made no visible movement; yet something in her attitude, the manner in which she held herself, seemed to bid him hold his peace, and this he noticed, and in noticing resented. "There," he muttered; "drop the Grand Duchess, will you? The brat is Thorold's; you know it, and so do I."

For a little space she stared as though uncertain she had heard aright, but the speech must have re-echoed in her ears; she had been sitting up, yet now as the echo reached her she drooped on the pillow and let her head fall back. In her arms the child still drowsed. And presently a tear rolled down her face, then another.

"Roland Mistrial, you have broken my heart at last."

That was all; the ultimate words even were scarcely audible; but the tears continued—the first succeeded by others, unstanched and undetained. Grief had claimed her as its own. She made no effort to rebel; she lay as though an agony had come from which no surcease can be. And as one tear after the other passed down and seared her face there was a silence so deathly, so tangible, and so convincing, that he needed no further sign from her to tell him that the charge was false. In all his intercourse with her, whatever cause of complaint there had been, never had he seen her weep before; and now at this unawaited evidence of the injustice and ignominy of his reproach he wished she would be defiant again, that he might argue and confute. But no word came from her—barely a sob; nothing, in fact, save these tears, which he had never seen before. And while he stood there, visited by the perplexity of him to whom the unawaited comes, unconsciously he went back to the wooing of her: he saw her clear eyes lifted in confidence to his own, he heard again the sweet confession of her love, he recalled the marks and tokens of her trust, and when for him she had left her father's house; he saw her ever, sweet by nature, tender-hearted, striving at each misdeed of his to show him that in her arms there was forgiveness still. And he recalled too the affronts he had put upon her, the baseness of his calculations, the selfishness of his life; he saw the misery he had inflicted, the affection he had beguiled, the hope he had tricked, and for climax there was this supreme reproach, of which he knew now no woman in all the world was less deserving than was she. And still the tears unstanched and undetained passed down and seared her cheeks; in the mortal wound he had aimed at her womanhood all else seemingly was forgot. She did not even move, and lay, her child tight clasped, the image of Maternity inhabited by Regret.

And such regret! Mistrial, unprompted, could divine it all. The regret of love misplaced, of illusions spent, the regret of harboring a ruffian and thinking him a knight. Yes, he could divine it all; and then, as such things can be, he grieved a moment for himself.

But soon the present returned. Justine still was weeping; he no longer saw her tears, he heard them. Surely she would forgive again. It could not be that everything had gone for naught. He would speak to her, plead if need were, and in the end she would yield. She must do that, he told himself, and he groped after some falsity that should palliate the offence. He would tell her that he had been drinking again; he would deny his own words, or, if necessary, he would insist she had not heard them aright. Indeed, there was nothing that might have weight with her which he was not ready and anxious to affirm. If she would but begin, if in some splendor of indignation such as he had beheld before she would rise up and upbraid him, his task would be diminished by half. Anything, indeed, would be better than this, and nothing could be worse; it was not Justine alone that the tears were carrying from him, it was the Dunellen millions as well. Oh, abysses of the human heart! As he queried with himself, at the very moment he was experiencing his first remorse, the old self returned, and it was less of the injury he had inflicted that he thought than of the counter-effect that injury might have on him. In the attempt to throttle the child he had been balked, yet of that attempt he believed Justine to be suspicionless. Other opportunities he would have in plenty; and even were it otherwise, the child was weakly, and croup might do its work. With the future for which he had striven, there, in the very palm of his hand, how was it possible that he should have made this misstep? But he could retrieve it, he told himself; he was a good actor, it was not too late. For a little while yet he could still support the mask, and, recalling the sentimental reveries of a moment before, the forerunner of a sneer came and loitered beneath the fringes of his mustache.

"Justine!" He moved a step or two to where she lay. "Justine—"

His voice was very low and penitent, but at the sound of it she seemed to shrink. "Could she know?" he wondered.

Then immediately, through the scantness of the apartment, he heard the outer bell resound. Enervated as he was, the interruption affected him like a barb. There was some one there whom he could vent his irritation on. He hurried to the hall, but a servant had preceded him. The door was open, and on the threshold Thorold stood.

Mistrial nodded—the nod of one who is about to throw his coat aside and roll his shirt-sleeves up. "Is it for your bill you come?" he asked.

Thorold hesitated, and his face grew very black. He affected, however, to ignore the taunt. He turned to the servant that still was waiting there. "Is my cousin at home?" he asked.

"She is," Mistrial announced, "but not to you."

"In that case," Thorold answered, "I must speak to someone in her stead."

Mistrial made a gesture, and the servant withdrew.

"I have to inform my cousin," Thorold continued, "that Mr. Metuchen came to me this evening and said that when my uncle died he was in debt—"

"Stuff and nonsense!"

"He asked me to come and acquaint Justine with the facts. They are here." With this Thorold produced a roll of papers. "Be good enough to explain to her," he added, "that this is the inventory of the estate." And, extending the documents to his host, he turned and disappeared.

In the cataleptic attitude of one standing to be photographed Mistrial listened to the retreating steps; he heard Thorold descend the stairs, cross the vestibule, and pass from the house. It seemed to him even that he caught the sound of his footfall on the pavement without. But presently that, too, had gone. He turned and looked down the hall. Justine's door was closed. Then at once, without seeking a seat, he fumbled through the papers that he held. The gas-jet above his head fell on the rigid lines. In the absence of collusion—and from whence should such a thing come?—in the absence of that, they were crystal in their clarity.

There were the assets. Shares in mines that did not exist, bonds of railways that were bankrupt, loans on Western swamps, the house on Madison Avenue, mortgaged to its utmost value, property on the Riverside, ditto. And so on and so forth till the eye wearied and the heart sickened of the catalogue. Then came the debit account. Amounts due to this estate, to that, and to the other, a list of items extending down an entire page of foolscap and extending over onto the next. There a balance had been struck. Instead of millions Honest Paul had left dishonor. Swindled by the living, he had swindled the dead.

"So much for trusting a man that bawls Amen in church," mused Mistrial.

As yet the completeness and amplitude of the disaster had not reached him. While he ran the papers over he feigned to himself that it was all some trick of Thorold's, one that he would presently see through and understand; and even as he grasped the fact that it was not a trick at all, that it was truth duly signed and attested, even then the disaster seemed remote, affecting him only after the manner of that wound which, received in the heat of battle, is unnoticed by the victim until its gravity makes him reel. Then at once in the distance the future on which he had counted faded and grew blank. Where it had been brilliant it was obscure, and that obscurity, increasing, walled back the horizon and reached up and extended from earth to sky. The papers fell from his nerveless hand, fright had visited him, and he wheeled like a rat surprised. Surely, he reflected, if safety there were or could be, that safety was with Justine.

In a moment he was at her door. He tried it. It was locked. He beat upon it and called aloud, "Justine."

No answer came. He bent his head and listened. Through the woodwork he could hear but the faintest rustle, and he called again, "Justine."

Then from within came the melody of her voice: "Who is it?"

"It is I," he answered, and straightened himself. It seemed odd to him she did not open the door at once. "I want a word with you," he added, after a pause. But still the door was locked.

"Justine," he called again, "do you not hear me? I want to speak to you."

Then through the slender woodwork at his side a whisper filtered, the dumb voice of one whom madness may have in charge.

"It is not to speak you come, it is to kill."

"Justine!" he cried. All the agony of his life he distilled into her name, "Justine!"

"You killed your child before, you shall not kill another now."

VI.

"City Hall!"

The brakemen were shouting the station through the emptiness of the "Elevated."

In the car in which Mistrial sat a drunken sailor lolled, and a pretty girl of the Sixth Avenue type was eating a confection. Above her, on a panel opposite, the advertisement of a cough remedy shone in blue; beyond was a particolored notice of tennis blazers: and, between them, a text from Mark, in black letters, jumped out from a background of white:

"What shall it profit a man, if he shall gain the whole world, and lose his own soul?"

During the journey from his home Mistrial had contemplated that text. Not continuously, however. For a little space his eyes had grazed the retreating throngs over which the train was hurrying, and had rested on the insufferable ugliness of the Bowery. Once, too, he had found himself staring at the girl who sat opposite, and once he had detected within him some envy of the sailor sprawling at her side. But, all the while, that text was with him, and to the jar of the car he repeated for refrain a paraphrase of his own: "How shall it damage a man if he lose his own soul and gain the whole world?"

How indeed? Surely he had tried. For three years the effort had been constant. It was because of it he had married, it was for this he had sought to throttle his child. What his failure had been, Dunellen's posthumous felony and Justine's ultimate reproach indistinctly yet clearly conveyed. No, the world was not gained; he had played his best and he had lost: he could never recover it now.

And as the brakeman bawled in his face, the paraphrase of the text was with him. He rose and passed from the car. Beneath he could discern a grass-plot of the City Park. In spite of the night it was visibly green. The sky was leaden as a military uniform that has been dragged through the mud. From a window of the Tribune Building came a vomit of vapor. And above in a steeple a clock marked twelve.

The stairway led him down to the street. For a moment he hesitated; the locality was unfamiliar. But a toll-gate attracted him; he approached it, paid a penny, and moved onto the bridge. There, he discovered that on either side of him were iron fences and iron rails; he was on the middle of the bridge, not at the side. A train shot by. He turned again and reissued from the gate.

On the corner was another entrance, and through it he saw a carriage pass. It was that way, he knew; and he would have followed the carriage, but a policeman touched him on the arm.

"Got a permit?"

Mistrial shook his head. Why should he have a permit? And, moved perhaps by the mute surprise his face expressed, the policeman explained that the ordinary pedestrian was allowed to cross only through the safeguards of the middle path.

"I will get a cab," he reflected, and for his convenience he discerned one loitering across the way. This he entered, gave an order to the driver, and presently, after paying another toll, rolled off the stonework on to wood.

He craned his neck. Just beyond, a column of stone rose inordinately to the lowering sky; he could see the water-front of the city; opposite was Brooklyn, and in front the lights of Staten Island glowed distantly and dim. The cab was moving slowly. He took some coin from his pocket, placed it on the seat, opened the door, and, stepping from the moving vehicle, looked at the driver. The latter, however, had not noticed him and was continuing his way leisurely over the bridge and on and into the night. Mistrial let him go undetained. He had work now to do, and it was necessary for him to do it quickly; at any moment another carriage might pass or some one happen that way.

Beneath, far down, a barge was moving. He could see the lights; they approached the bridge and vanished within it. The railing, now, he saw was too high to vault, and moreover there was a bar above it that might interfere. He tossed his hat aside and clambered on the iron rail.

"You'll get six months for that," some one was crying.

But to the threat Mistrial paid no heed. He had crossed the rail, his hands relaxed, and just as he dropped straight down to the river below, he could see a policeman, his club uplifted, hanging over the fence, promising him the pleasures of imprisonment. Such was his last glimpse of earth. A multitude of lights danced before his eyes; every nerve in his body tingled; his ears were filled with sudden sounds; he felt himself incased in ice; then something snapped, and all was blank.

The next day a rumor of the suicide was bruited through the clubs.

"What do you think of it, Jones?" Yarde asked.

The novelist plucked at his beard. There were times when he himself did not know what he thought. In this instance, however, he had already learned of the disaster that had overtaken the Dunellen estate, and weaving two and two sagaciously together, he answered with a shrug.

"What do I think of it? I think he died like a man who knew how to live"—an epitaph which pleased him so much that he got his card-case out and wrote it down.

THE END.

Milton Keynes UK
Ingram Content Group UK Ltd.
UKHW051855240424
441687UK00011B/360